# EARTH'S LAIR
EARTH'S MAGIC BOOK 2

EVE LANGLAIS

Copyright © 2021 /2022 Eve Langlais

Cover by Addictive Covers © 2021/2022

Produced in Canada

Published by Eve Langlais

http://www.EveLanglais.com

Canadian Intellectual Property Office Registration Number : XXX

E-ISBN: 978 177 384 3155

Print ISBN: 978 177 384 3162

**ALL RIGHTS RESERVED**

This book is a work of fiction and the characters, events and dialogue found within the story are of the author's imagination and are not to be construed as real. Any resemblance to actual events or persons, either living or deceased, is completely coincidental.

No part of this book may be reproduced or shared in any form or by any means, electronic or mechanical, including but not limited to digital copying, file sharing, audio recording, email and printing without permission in writing from the author.

# PROLOGUE

*In a world where magic was allowed to flourish and secrets remained hidden for a reason...*

The house settled into a quiet slumber with only the ticking of the clock in the hall as Mama and Papa went to bed. They thought me asleep already. Technically, I should have been. Only a new book by the king of horror had been released, and I hid under the covers reading it.

I shivered in delight as evil won over good and sighed happily as I placed the finished paperback on my nightstand. I'd take bad winning the day when heroes were dumb.

Don't go in the haunted house at night on Halloween.

Do not take a shower when the power goes out.

Don't go anywhere without a gun. Or an axe. Or something with a sharp blade. I kept my baseball bat tucked between the bed and nightstand and a steak knife under my pillow. Mom had given up trying to take it back. As if she could argue with my logic—*What if the apocalypse hits and I get killed by a zombie because I only have a pillow to defend myself?* It should be noted I'd never been attacked, but I would be ready if and when it happened.

As I settled into my pillow, my mind still whirling with the story, I stared at my window, the drapes open so I could see outside. Only rather than a night sky with twinkling stars, it erupted with gold and silver light.

Cool. Even more fascinating, the light appeared to originate from the ground and not the heavens above.

I didn't think twice. I jammed my feet into my running shoes and grabbed a sweater before climbing out my window. Not the first time I'd slipped out.

The explosion of lights wasn't on my parents' farm, but I could tell where they came from. I rode my bike up the road to the property adjoining ours, about a mile away. The illumination brightened, and

I'd have sworn I heard singing, beautiful and haunting, no actual words just a melody.

As I reached the driveway for the Samsons' property, I braked in the gravel and listened, eyes half closed. What was making that beautiful sound and light?

It abruptly ceased.

Darkness fell harshly, as did the silence. Tears filled my eyes at the loss.

What happened? I put my feet on the pedals, ready to head down that driveway to find out, when a figure strode from the shadows.

"Where da fuck you goin', girl?"

I knew that voice. Leroy Samson. Son of Earl Samson, owner of the land beside our farm. "Hello, Mr. Samson." He looked a lot like his dad if younger. Always scowling and cradling a gun. Neither liked people.

"Go away."

"Sorry to bug you. I saw a light."

"No light."

I frowned at the obvious lie. "There was, from over there." I pointed past him. "And I heard singing, too."

"No, you didn't. You heard nothing. Do you hear me? Nothing," he enunciated before glancing behind him. "Git before my father sees you and gets pissed."

Why would he get mad? I'd done nothing wrong.

Still, it was late, dark, and I'd come alone. Perhaps I should leave before Mr. Samson lived up to his reputation among the kids of being a killer who dropped the bodies of his victims down a well. Whose body, the rumors didn't say. We just knew there was something off about the Samsons.

I pedaled home, keeping an eye on the sky, listening for music. It was almost thirty years before I heard it again.

# CHAPTER ONE

The flame on my lighter danced in the gentle afternoon breeze. The old Zippo— passed down to me by my grandfather, who used to smoke cigars, puffing hard on them while he verbally replayed his youth—remained lit despite the wind. Quality design at work.

I lit the end of the long fuse and ran for the grassy knoll. I ducked behind its solid girth and wrapped my arms over my head as I counted down.

*Ten, nine, eight...*

Technically, I had no idea how long it would take for the spark to light the –

*Kaboom!*

The ground underfoot trembled as the dynamite I'd planted exploded. The end result? A shower of rocks and dirt.

Once the intentional apocalypse ended, I stood. Dust hung in the air, making me glad I'd remembered to wear my goggles. The last time I'd forgotten and ended up in the emergency department with a doctor chiding me as he removed debris from my eye. Very unpleasant, although I did enjoy wearing the eye patch as it healed and shouting, "Arrr, matey," at anyone who stared in my direction. I really didn't give a rat's ass what people thought of me.

Some women waited to hit their forties to ooze confidence. I wrangled mine at an earlier age. No shame. No filter. No fucks to give.

As I trudged in my yellow galoshes, decorated with red devil duckies, toward the pile of boulders I'd decimated, I noted the recently created stumps spread out over the acre I'd been clearing for the last two weeks as part of my farm expansion.

You were looking at a bona fide farmer. Me, Annie Jenner, sole owner of the farm I'd inherited before the age of twenty. A property and business I chose to keep despite the naysayers—also known as that asshole at the bank—trying to convince me to sell it to developers.

*"You're only nineteen. You don't really want to tie yourself to a farm. You should go to school in another state. See the world."*

I could see the world on television. I refused to give up the farm that had been passed down in my family for several generations. I did leave for a while to attend college the next state over. I wanted an education. Running a successful farm was more than feeding animals and planting seeds. Just ask my daddy. It was hard work and the reason he chose to ditch farming for a job in town. Daddy told me he wasn't a farmer, despite the fact his dad and his dad's dad were.

It must have skipped a generation because I loved the land. While I didn't have a magical green thumb like my best friend, I knew how to get things to flourish. Plants or animals. It took me a while—working full-time in town and then part-time as I got the farm going—before I could make the switch. Even then, I worked on a small scale.

A recent zombie invasion—which I'd helped prevent along with my BFF Mindy, a goblin named Mungo, and some dude working for the Cryptid Authority—had left me with empty barns and paddocks. A necromancer had zombified all my livestock as part of her devious plot to take over the world, which failed, in part due to me.

After the fact, it was a fight to get the insurance company to pay out. Good thing social media had recorded video evidence to prove my claim. Nothing like showing the adjustor one of my zombie cows rampaging down the street, chasing school children, to get him to admit maybe I was telling the truth. As if I'd lie about something like that. The vindication of winning almost offset my annoyance that my previous claim—when aliens beamed up my stud bull—failed to pay out. Apparently, the tiny burned circle left behind wasn't proof of little green men.

Anyhow, back to the farming. Given my success, it was time to expand, which gave me a good excuse to blow shit up.

I tromped through the newly created field, noting all the hunks of rocks strewn from one end to the other. Others might have been daunted by all the stone. I saw what it would become: the rocky liner for the new pond I'd been meaning to put in. Tomorrow, I'd hook up the landscape rake to my tractor and drag the debris into a pile.

As the dust settled, I got a clearer look at the remains of the mound I'd blown up using the dynamite bought off the back of a truck from a guy who also dealt in fireworks. Technically, illegal, but the legit places couldn't beat his price. Add in the fact I didn't have to apply for a permit and I could explode shit to my heart's content. The advantage of living in the boonies. The one time someone came asking if I'd heard or felt anything strange, I'd managed wide-eyed awe about the savage storm that blew through. The bylaw idiot bought it, although that might have had something to do with the jar of moonshine I sent him off with.

The spot I'd exploded still showed a layer of rocks that would require removal. Some were small enough I could toss them by hand, exposing the larger chunks remaining. One more blast would have cleared it, but then I'd have a crater in the ground that I'd have to fill. Less work to yank them free with my tractor.

Thinking of work had me wondering about the odd pile of rocks hidden in the previously gnarly forest. A possibly manmade tower of stone, perhaps some kind of totem or marker or a cairn. Would I find some skeletons?

I should be so lucky. What I wouldn't give for something exciting to happen to me. I mean, yeah, my animals being turned into zombies to panic the populace was kind of cool, and helping my BFF track down a necromancer to end her reign of evil was epic. However, I was only a sidekick to her illustrious battle. Mindy was the one to save the day and get the guy. Lucky bitch. Good thing we were best friends or I'd have totally made a play for her boyfriend, Reiver. I did have a thing for bad boys, even though it got me into trouble.

Ask anyone, they'd tell you I had bad taste in men. Always had. But none as horrible as the first to break my heart. If that bastard ever showed his face, I'd smash it in. But he'd left, a coward in the night, with no care to the damage he'd wrought to me: mind and body.

As I walked around the remaining rocks I'd have to yank and move, a bleat from behind had me turning to see Jilly, a recently adopted pygmy goat with a short but sharp horn between her eyes, floppy ears, and no nipples despite being female. I couldn't have even said why I took her in given she'd never produce milk or ever give me edible or sellable meat. And before you act shocked, keep in mind, I was a farmer. Everything on my farm served a purpose. Crops for food. Animals, too. I didn't do pets. The cats in my barn? They were for mice. The dogs? Herding my sheep.

But Jilly, the oddball goat? She'd been part of the assets of an estate auction. The guy beside me started bidding on her, joking to his companion she'd make an excellent circus freak. It bothered me enough that I overpaid for her clumsy butt.

You know how goats are usually agile climbers? Not my Jilly. She tripped over her own legs. Got her single horn stuck in everything. And, yes, despite that bony protrusion and lack of boobies, she was most definitely female. A mishmash of parts that didn't fit in anywhere.

Like me.

I'd grown up with people making fun of my appearance. My hair was a wild, curly mess that, when brushed, poofed out into a massive halo. I didn't have the patience to braid it and rather liked it au natural. My skin color wasn't dark enough for some, too light for others. Adding in freckles and the way I dressed for comfort rather than style had led to me being teased and bullied. The only people who accepted me for me were my parents and Mindy.

Not that I cared what people thought. I took pride in my unique style. All that to say I looked at Jilly and saw myself. Awkward, not fitting in anywhere, but going about blithely confident and happy because I wasn't about to let anyone make me believe I wasn't worthy.

"What are you doing here, fuzz butt?" I chided.

She took that as an invitation and came trotting as fast as her four legs could carry her, which involved a sway to the left, a wobble to the right, and an almost face plant.

"Careful," I warned as she only barely missed stepping in a rut that might have hurt her leg.

The squeak uttered by Jilly had me snorting.

"Don't give me attitude. I've seen you in action, fuzz butt."

As if to prove me wrong, she danced atop the pile of rocks left behind, and almost managed to look graceful until she slid off a stone and crashed, muzzle first. As if that stopped her. She popped right back up, tongue lolling in a smile.

I shook my head. "Such an idiot." But a cute one. "Come on, oh four-legged accident waiting to happen. Let's go get the tractor." Because the ATV I rode out on didn't have the right attachments to do the work needed.

Jilly hopped on the back, shaking with excitement. She loved going for rides, usually with her tongue hanging and ears flopping around, because those suckers refused to stand up straight.

Once we reached the farm, she ran lopsided back for the barn. I followed her pink-pajama butt, because, in my world, pet goats belonged in pajamas.

At Christmas, she'd worn a set with flashing Christmas lights along with a matching strand around her tiny horn. It should be noted I'd worn something of the same fabric to a Christmas party at my best friend's, which caused Mindy's boyfriend, Reiver, to exclaim, "What the ever-loving fuck are you wearing?" Whereas Mindy just nodded and said, "At least it's not as bad as the year she came dressed as a roasted turkey." Replete with a gravy-scented perfume. To get me back, Mindy made me healthy muffins for a week. Her cruelty knew no bounds.

As I strode past a paddock, I waved to Benji, one of the new farmhands, who was dumping some vegetable scraps and barley into a trough for the pigs. The scrawny suckers would need fattening before they'd turn into bacon and pork chops.

Mmm.

Don't act shocked. Remember what I said about judging? Food was a necessity. And while veganism might be fine for some folks, I would always be a girl who loved her protein, unlike my vegetarian BFF who would only eat plants and ethically sourced eggs and dairy.

It wasn't long before I rumbled the tractor back to my newly created field. The previous week I'd removed the trees I'd felled, the copse I'd taken down old and gnarly. The trunks twisted and stunted, the branches barely producing leaves. It made me question the quality of the soil, only analysis of it by a lab I trusted indicated the perfect balance. Despite the appearance of the trees, this dirt was made for growing stuff.

Before I'd bought the acres of land bordering

mine, I'd often imagined those woods were haunted. The previous owner, Leroy Samson, had reinforced that belief with his barbed wire fence and no trespassing signs. He'd often been seen, shotgun cradled in his arms, guarding his borders. Against what, no one ever knew.

Poor Samson got eaten by zombies the night my animals were kidnapped by the necromancer. When his property went up for auction a few months later, not only did I buy Jilly at the estate part of the sale but I snatched up the property, too. I had dreams of my farm expanding enough to eventually allow for me to raise alpacas and ostriches. The latter's eggs were worth a fortune to chefs.

The moment the adjoining property became mine, the first thing I did was tear down the fence separating the land. I followed up by taking a chain saw to those useless trees, so dry and rotted they wouldn't even make decent firewood. As I exposed the land long hidden from the sun, I discovered the tall mound of lichen-covered boulders, too big to easily move.

Okay, not entirely true. I could have hired a crane to relocate them, but personally, I preferred blowing shit up.

Jilly sat in a lined metal basket welded to the back of my seat on the tractor. She bleated in excitement as we rumbled our way onto the field. As I reached the blast zone, I lowered the bucket to scoop the remaining chunks of rock. One by one, I removed them, trundling across the field to the edge of a ravine that led to a creek—more like a raging river this time of the year, just after the winter melt.

The rocks went tumbling over the edge, a no-no that would get me in trouble if the town inspectors ever found out. They wouldn't because then I might stop giving them deals on farm-fresh produce.

The rubble diminished until only one massive slab remained. It was almost square in shape and flat to the ground. And me without any more dynamite.

I improvised and slammed the bucket down on it. The rock cracked, but before I could think of scooping the pieces, the chunks fell into the chasm that opened beneath it!

## CHAPTER
# TWO

HOLY FUCKING SHIT! I'D NOT EXPECTED TO FIND A HOLE IN the middle of my new field.

I hopped off my tractor, thudding hard on the ground. My knees complained. Might be time to get into Grandma's recipe books and make some of her special salve—minus the bat wing and eye of newt, which she'd once drunkenly confided was to screw with people.

I headed for the edge of the opening in the ground, halted, and wondered at the stability of the ground. I glanced at the tractor, but it was fine. And I'd had to slam the rock pretty darned hard to get it to crack.

Fuck it. I moved for the hole and noticed the stone blocks framing the opening. I blinked, but the clean-cut rock remained, forming a border and...

Wait a second, were those stairs? Oh, hell yes, there were stairs going down.

Excitement threatened to burst my body into gooey meat chunks as I discovered an honest to God—

Um. What had I found? No idea other than it was interesting as fuck. And me without a flashlight.

"Dammit!" I didn't have a damned thing to light my path because my dumb ass forgot to charge my phone and it had less than five percent. I eyed the direction of my farm. A long trip back. I should try improvising first. After all, I did have my lighter. I'd fabricate a torch to take a peek.

Before I could scavenge for a proper hunk of wood, Jilly stood on the top step and gazed with curiosity at the darkness below.

"Don't go down there." Who knew what kind of hazards might await my clumsy goat.

Jilly nodded as if in agreement, which led to her losing her balance, and next thing I knew, she went tumbling down.

So of course, I went after her. No torch, nothing but a hint of panic.

The waning afternoon light didn't penetrate far, only enough for me to realize the stairs descended a fair bit. When visibility became poor, I put my hand on the stone wall, surprised to find it warm rather than cool to the touch. The smooth stone possessed regularly spaced seams, showcasing a straight and solidly built place. But why? For what?

My goat let out a plaintive bleat that didn't echo one bit, as if the place absorbed all sound.

"I'm coming, fluff butt. Don't move." Here was hoping she'd listen this time.

I lost count of how many steps I'd gone down before I realized either my eyes had adjusted to the darkness or it was getting lighter below. Soon I could make out the stone stairs and the walls. The source of light appeared to be coming from the landing that marked the end of my descent, not that I saw any bulbs, candles, or even torches. Nothing to actually cause anything to illuminate, and yet I could see. I also found my dumb goat.

Jilly stood in front of a massive stone door etched with a giant eye framed in zig-zag lashes.

"Cool," I breathed as I stood in awe before the portal that was at least ten feet tall. No handle to open it, nor even a keyhole to unlock it. What lay behind? Ancient temple? Crypt? Treasure chamber? Did it matter? In this moment, I was Indiana Jane. Intrepid explorer. I just needed a hat and a whip.

Instead, I had muddy overalls, rubber galoshes, and a goat who thought it a good idea to lick the door.

"I don't think that's going to open it, fluff butt," I advised my pet.

Jilly bleated and continued to lavish the stone portal with her copious spit. Which didn't do a thing.

For a second, I thought of running to get some more dynamite, but blowing up a random pile of rocks was one thing. Even I knew better than to destroy something this historic. This type of mystery should be reported to those equipped for handle it. The problem being, if I told anyone about it, they'd probably declare my field off-limits. Steal whatever lay on the other side. Ruin my chance at a proper adventure.

Ugh. What to do?

I put a hand against the stone. Icy cold in comparison to the walls in the stairwell.

Maybe the cairn of rocks had hidden this staircase and entrance for a reason. What if what hid beyond was evil? A portal to somewhere really bad? It would explain my ornery neighbor's stance on trespassing. Did I want to accidentally unleash the forces of Hell, or worse, upon my world?

Sigh. I could hear echoes of my best friend in that worry. A younger me would have said fuck it, open the door! However, I liked to think at almost forty I'd matured enough to know better.

"Guess I need to be responsible about this." I grimaced. Adulting sucked.

Before heading back up, I rubbed the door, groped it, knocked on it. I drew the line at lavishing it with spit like my goat. When it became obvious I wouldn't be opening it, I snapped my fingers. "Let's go, fluff butt. Feels like dinnertime to me."

*"Blaaaah,"* Jilly agreed.

We made the long trip back up the stairs, and I slouched in the tractor going home. Tired legs couldn't trump my excitement over my find.

A mystery. In my field. I immediately called Mindy to tell her all about it.

"I found a secret set of stairs going deep underground!" My exuberant version of hello.

"Where?"

"Old Samson's place. That new field I've been clearing. I think I might have found some kind of tomb. You should see the size of the door at the bottom. It's huge."

"Please tell me you didn't open it," Mindy exclaimed.

"I didn't." Then a whiny, "Because it's locked or something."

"Thank cupcake." Mindy sighed in relief.

"What's the worst that could have happened?"

"Toxic gases. Supernatural prison..." Mindy had

a list that ended with the end of life as we knew it. "Promise me you'll call a pro to look at it before you do anything."

I sighed. Mindy sure had a way of guilting a person into being responsible. "Fine. I'll get someone out here to check it out."

I hung up, and then, before I could change my mind, I made the other call.

"Cryptid Historical Society, how may I direct your call?" a perky feminine voice asked.

"Hey, so I'm not sure if you're interested, but figured I should call 'cause I found something on my property."

"Object or body?"

"More like secret underground stone passage with a giant locked door engraved with an eyeball."

A pause followed my words before the receptionist with a montone voice recovered with a huff. "Please hold."

I didn't hold for long. The next person I spoke to could barely contain their excitement at my description.

"Don't tell anyone what you've found, or do anything with it," they admonished.

I agreed, only because my legs told me I could fuck off if I thought they were doing that trek up and down those stairs again anytime soon.

That night I went to bed and had a dream. I dreamed of the night I saw the light in the sky and heard singing. But this time, the show didn't abruptly halt and I kept riding down Samson's driveway toward that light, which came from a hole in the ground that looked an awful lot like the one in my field.

As I got closer, the singing became clear.

*"Save me. Save me."*

How? I had no idea who asked, just that I wanted desperately to help that voice. As I reached the light, I tried to look down, squinting against the brightness.

I reached, head turned to the side, trying to avoid closing my eyes. Judging by the dry scaly texture, what grabbed my ankle wasn't human.

The realization shot me out of sleep. I woke and sat up in my bed, sweaty and gross. Scared.

Which kind of freaked me out. How could I be scared of a silly dream?

A hot shower and breakfast did much to reassure so that by the time the handsome stranger arrived, I was feeling in fine form.

So fine that when I opened the door, I drawled, "Please tell me you were sent here to stud."

# CHAPTER
# THREE

I'd propositioned a stranger. It was bad even by my lax terms. "I'm sorry. I didn't mean that how it sounded." Remember how I claimed I was in my don't-give-a-fuck years? It should also be noted I had some weird social awkwardness when it came to cute guys. As in I said the stupidest things.

To his credit, his jaw didn't drop, but he did frown. "Are you Annie Jenner?"

"Who's asking?" I eyeballed him more closely, looking past his handsome face to the rest of him. A blond hunk wearing tan cargo-pocket chinos and a long-sleeve shirt layered with a battered leather coat, but no hat or whip. Instead, he held a satchel. Had to be the historical society fellow.

As for my outfit? I'd opted for leggings patterned with pumpkins and a bright green sweatshirt that had a smiling vegetable exclaiming, "So excited, I pea-ed." Add in hair that chose to pretend there was humidity and it completed my look.

"I'm Annie. You must be the CHS fellow." I held out my hand for a shake. He replied with a strong grip, and I noticed the callouses on his hand. Not just a book nerd.

"I'm Howard Cunningham. Archeologist and historian. I hear you found something interesting."

"Fuck yeah I did," I blurted out, only to slam my lips shut. Me and my big potty mouth.

His eyes crinkled at the corners when he smiled. "Don't contain your excitement on my account. I'd say it was warranted."

"It was pretty cool." I'd not been able to stop thinking about the mysterious door. I wish I'd thought to grab my dying phone before I'd gone down after Jilly. Wished my legs would have agreed to another trip last night.

"Can you describe it for me? I'd like to hear about it in your own words and not those relayed by my colleague."

"Sure." I went into an account that didn't include dynamite or my illegal dumping of rocks and breaking of a possible historical monument.

He eyed me with intent interest the entire time.

When I finished my tale by describing the eye on the door, he said politely, "May I see?"

I nodded. "It's a fair distance, though. Tractor's in use by Karra, one of my farmhands. She's prepping the delta pasture, so we'll take the ATV. It will be faster than on foot."

"That sounds perfect."

Wait until he realized he'd be riding behind me.

My machine was gassed and ready to go with a small bag of tools—that might have included a sledgehammer—strapped to the rack at the back. You know, in case we needed to bust our way in. That door could not stay closed forever. I had to know what lay behind it. *Needed* to see.

I'll admit that strong desire worried me. I'd been around enough weird stuff to admit it might be artificial, a compulsion triggered perhaps by some kind of spell around the door. At the same time, who wouldn't want to know what lay behind the mysterious portal? Maybe it was the tomb of some ancient queen with all kinds of expensive jewels.

"I assume that's our ride?" Mr. Cunningham stood by my side, making me realize he was many inches taller than me.

A shiver of delight hit because I did so love a man who made me feel dainty. Mock me all you want. I might be a strong, independent woman, but sometimes I wanted to let go. Be the fucking damsel in distress. The one on the bottom making him do all the work.

"Hope you don't mind getting a little muddy."

"It wouldn't be a real discovery without some dirt. Where do you keep the spare helmet?"

The fact he asked almost made me cringe. "We don't have any." I shrugged. "When you're used to running machines on a daily basis, you kind of forget about using them. We know better than to drive like idiots." Most of the time. The exception being that time Mavis, my damned cow who survived the zombie apocalypse by being at the vet, got pregnant and turned ugly. Mooing as if possessed, the cow chased me out of her pasture at a speed that almost killed me. "Will the lack of helmet be a problem?"

"Given your head appears nicely shaped and you've not lost your wits, I shall trust to your expertise. Although I do wonder where I'll be sitting."

I did my best to not smirk as I said, "Behind me."

"Will there be enough room?" He inclined his head as he asked what turned out to be a valid question, given Jilly, wearing her cloudy pajamas, had claimed the passenger seat of the ATV.

My little goat bleated.

"Get down, fluff butt." I waved my hands to shoo

her. Jilly shook her horn in reply. I swear at times she understood me.

"Is that a goat?" Cunningham asked.

"Yup. Although I don't think she realizes it. She likes going for rides."

"There's room enough for us both if she's okay being in my lap." A surprising offer. He approached my goat and reached, fingers extended for Jilly to sniff.

Bold, but, at the same time, cautious.

Jilly froze before her nose twitched. She went through a disjointed shiver before making a noise and butting into his hand. Given she also loved my cactus and required me pulling the needles out one by one, I sometimes wondered about her judgement.

"Well, that took all of five seconds," I muttered as the traitor decided she now loved the archeologist. Given she liked few people—only me and Mindy were allowed to touch her—this raised the hot dude in my estimation.

He tucked his satchel on the front rack of my ride, using the bungies to hold it. Then held out his hands.

"May I?" he asked my goat, and Jilly graciously allowed him to scoop her before he seated himself on the back, a pajamaed goat in his lap. It was ridiculously cute. Better than a man and a baby. Way better because this was within my reach. I just had to act cool. Sexy. Other women did it all the time.

I went to swing my leg over the ATV and felt the ping as a stitch ripped. I jerked my leg down too fast, lost my balance, and fell on my ass.

Oof. There went graceful. I popped to my feet as Cunningham graciously pretended not to see my lapse.

"I forgot something. Be right back." I raced into my house, changed my pants to ones without a hole—I couldn't do anything about the fact he'd probably notice I now wore overalls—then raced back outside.

"Shall we?" I hopped on, this time without mishap, while, at the same time, chastising myself for not ignoring the tear in my leggings. Whatever happened to my rule, take me as I was, ripped pants and all? As I raced for forty, still alone, it occurred to me I might have to relax some of my conditions.

Cunningham did not grab hold of me during the ride over to the mystery doorway. I tried to get him to, taking some of the most jostle-filled options on the path over, like riding through the furrowed field, making us bounce. He didn't scream or place his big, manly hands on my body. He held Jilly cradled to his chest.

Fuck him for being an adorable gentleman.

When we arrived by the hole and I slowed to a stop, he finally leaned close to say, "Thank you, Ms. Jenner."

Butterflies exploded in me like I'd not felt in a long time. "You're welcome. Call me Annie."

"Only if you'll do the same."

"Sure, Annie." I giggled. Giggled at my own super lame joke.

"Actually it's—"

"Howard," I interrupted. "I remember." I tried to not hear a quack as I thought of Howard the Duck. *Don't Google it. Dear God. You searched it, didn't you? I warned you.*

He grimaced. "Only my mother ever calls me that. My friends call me Ward." A much sexier appellation. "That was a fun ride," he added as he slid off the back of the ATV with my goat. He did me the pleasure of bending over to put Jilly on the ground. Nice view.

I knew what kind of ride I'd prefer to give him. He'd be doing more than thanking me. He'd be cross-eyed, panting, and limp as a noodle.

I took my sex seriously and strenuously.

The man straightened, and my goat gazed upward, showering him with adoration. We apparently had the same taste in men. I wasn't sure what that said about me.

Ward removed his satchel from the ATV and pulled out some boring stuff. Camera. Measuring tape. No bullwhip, pistol, or a metal censer swinging on a chain, belching smoke to combat possible evil spirits in the area. He even erected a tripod for the camera and began snapping shots. A few clicks in, the questions began.

"This area appears recently cleared."

"Because I only started clearing this patch after the spring melt. I bought the place bordering mine in winter. Soon as the ground thawed, I began expanding." I had plans for Earth's Bounty, the name I'd given my organic and ethical farm.

"I'm assuming there were trees before."

"Yup. They surrounded this whole area." I swung my arms.

"It would explain why your discovery remained hidden for so long. The report you called in indicated there used to be rocks covering the aperture?"

"A huge pile of them."

"Natural in formation?"

"Yes and no. I mean, I doubt Mother Earth dropped them in a neat pile, but at the same time, they weren't fitted or mortared into place. Like it was just a cone-shaped tower that started out wide at the bottom and thinned at the top. All kinds of rocks, except for the one at the very bottom. It was square and flat in shape."

"Did it bear any symbols or signs?"

"Nope." Not that I'd seen, but then again, I'd not really examined it.

"How did you remove the rocks?"

"Tractor." I omitted the dynamite step, but he had to know given he glanced to the sides and couldn't help but see the shards littering the field. I hoped he didn't ask what I'd done with the bigger chunks. In retrospect, this might get me in trouble. Think they'd believe I'd lost them all by accident?

"It appears some of the stone fell into the hole." He pointed.

"The last one broke when I tried to remove it with my tractor." I waited for an admonishment that didn't come. What did a girl have to do in order to get put over his knee for a spanking?

"A good thing you thought to move it, or we might have never found this historical site." Ward knelt by the stone edging the descent into the ground. "How far do the stairs go?"

"Far enough." My legs remained sore from my single climb the day before.

Ward took more images, this time moving around with his camera, followed by measurements, dictating the results into his phone, along with observations. Boring. When would we get to the exciting part where we opened the door? Or celebrated the find with sex?

Ward removed a large flashlight from his satchel.

"You won't need that. There's light at the bottom," I advised.

"So you mentioned, but the rest of the journey was in the dark, correct?" At my nod, he said, "Then best we bring a few things just in case."

Good point. He also brought a bag that he said contained bottles and bags to take samples and even a portable ultraviolet lamp.

When Ward had packed a knapsack with what he deemed essentials, he flicked a switch and aimed a flashlight at the hole. The bright beam did much to dispel the gloom, revealing stone walls and stairs, some littered with the broken rock from the day before. "Ready to go?"

"Am I ever." I practically rubbed my hands in glee—my thighs, on the other hand, groaned. Let them bitch. This was my find. My mystery. No way would I sit this one out. My goat on the other hand chose to remain atop.

I headed down the steps, avoiding the stone that had landed on the first few when I broke the barrier.

Having gone up and down once already, and with an actual light this time, I didn't hesitate. I skipped—okay, more liked glomped, each galosh hitting the stone hard.

Ward didn't say much as he swung his light side to side. Occasionally he stopped and took a picture of the receding square of daylight that marked the entrance. We went deep enough we lost sight of it and only had his tiny, bobbing light to mark our path. He kept up with my pace as I went down the straight path. Like literally, straight down. An odd choice. Large staircases usually spiraled.

Who knew how long or how far in the descent the light began to flicker, but a few more steps and it went out completely.

"That's weird." Usually a weak battery meant fading illumination. Not instant death.

"Odd. It was fully charged before we left," Ward mumbled as he clicked the on/off switch and then resorted to slapping it. Nada.

"Hold on. We'll use my phone's flashlight." I'd remembered to charge and bring it this time. I pulled it from my pocket and, despite how much I squashed the power button, it wouldn't come on. "My battery is dead, too."

"Interesting," Ward mused aloud. "It appears

there is a phenomenon messing with electronics. How far are we from the bottom?"

"Don't know, but I'm going to guess close. And is it me, or can you see a little?"

He hesitated before saying, "You're right. The darkness isn't absolute. Shall we continue?"

We continued down at a quicker pace, and the stairwell brightened.

"There's no visible light source," Ward mentioned as we neared the landing, the end of our journey down.

"Not that I found. And I think it's getting brighter. First time I came down, it wasn't this noticeable." The brightness around us showed off the intricate stonework, fancier than I'd realized the day before, with the stone parts forming swirling patterns.

Ward placed his hand against the stone wall. "There is magic here."

"No shit," I muttered. Even my mostly human butt could feel it. My mom had some elf genetics, but they appeared to have skipped me. As for Dad, no cryptid at all according to him.

"Here is the door you mentioned. A most incredible find." Awe filled Ward's words as he stood in front of the portal with its giant carving.

"Do you know what this place is?"

"Yes, although it was thought to be a myth. If I'm correct, though, then you have found the tomb of Satrina."

"Who?"

"Satrina, the last dragon."

## CHAPTER
# FOUR

Wait, did he say what I thought he'd said? "Um, can you repeat that?"

"I believe you found Satrina's Lair. The last living dragon."

That was unexpected and exciting. I squealed. "Seriously? They existed?"

"Yes, a long time ago. Beautiful creatures, but territorial and violent. As humanity expanded, there were clashes that led to the dragons' extinction. All but one. Satrina, the wiliest and strongest of them all. It is said she hid from humanity, evaded them, and plotted her return to power."

"Are you trying to tell me she's behind that door?" I eyed it. If the door were built to accommodate a dragon, that made it big. Bigger than me, but at the same time, the stairs weren't very large, indicating size might vary. Either way, I wished I'd brought a weapon. Pitchfork for poking. Rifle. Just about anything but my makeshift flamethrower would have worked against a giant, fire-breathing lizard.

"Doubtful this is her resting place given she lived in Europe. Then again, who knows?" Ward shrugged. "She disappeared, never to be seen again. Some assumed humanity got to her. Others that she died of a lonely heart." Ward traced his fingers on the wall, skimming the etched pattern.

"What do you think?" I asked.

"I think the answer doesn't matter since she's long dead. You should be asking a different question. What is one thing we all know of dragons?" He turned his gaze on me, waiting a reply.

My brain farted before I managed to sputter, "Dragons were big, flying lizards. Long tails. Scales. Some could breathe fire."

"Yes, and?"

It took some concentration to pull up the bits I knew. "Pictures show they had short arms like a T-rex. In some stories, they could shapeshift, too."

"All yes, but still not the correct reply. Dragons as a species were varied in their attributes, but they all had one thing in common." He paused, and when

I eyed him blankly, he whispered, "Every single one possessed a hoard."

I'll admit my first thought was the other kind of horde, the ones that were bearded and wearing animal fur, screaming as they attacked. Then a light bulb blinded me as I realized what he actually meant.

"You're talking about a treasure."

"Not just any treasure. Satrina, as the oldest and most powerful dragon, amassed a fortune, not just in precious metals and jewels. Scrolls with secrets and magic. Enchanted armor and weapons…"

The more things he listed, the more I wet my panties. Like literally. And I couldn't contain my excitement as I blurted out, "That is the hottest thing a guy has ever said to me."

Ward's lips quirked as he quipped, "Then you're not talking to the right guys."

"Know any? Right guys, that is." Cringeworthy yes, but I didn't know any other way than blunt.

Ward didn't recoil as he drawled, "I just might."

Well, that answered one question. I'd be sleeping with Mr. Sexy Archeologist. Just not here. I was getting too old for stair sex. I preferred a bed. "You'll have to tell me all about that guy later. I don't know about you, but I want to know if there's treasure behind that door."

"It's a date." He winked and turned back the portal. "This symbol"—his fingers skimmed over it—"was Satrina's personal crest."

"So she built this place?" I asked.

"No."

"I'm confused. If she didn't make this place, then what makes you think her treasure is here?"

"Because the symbol is a warning. Can't you feel it? The magical nudge telling us about the danger."

I blinked because I didn't feel a damned thing. "My magical radar must be broken because all I want is to open the door." Then because impulse was my thing, "I can run back up and get the sledgehammer if you want." I'd suffer the pain in my thighs if I could get inside.

"You truly do want to enter. Interesting." He eyed me for a second before returning to frown at the locked portal. "I wonder why it interacts with us differently?"

"Maybe it's a girl thing. Jilly liked the door a lot, too."

That arched his brow. "You brought your goat down?"

"More like she fell and I went to rescue her."

"A brave thing to do. Lucky for you, the spells protecting the approach are of benign design. In place to warn and repel." He traced the seam in the wall. "The stonework is dwarven, but the spell most definitely elven."

This got better and better. "How can you tell?"

"It's what I do for a living." He didn't rebuke me for my dumbness.

In retrospect, a stupid question. "The elves and dwarves hid the dragon's hoard?"

"Hid, yes, but they also wanted it forgotten. Left alone. This is meant to keep people away."

"Didn't stop me, or you."

"You have no idea of the effort it is taking to not turn around," he muttered through gritted teeth. When I started looking, I noted the strain in the crease around his eyes, the set of his jaw.

He fought his urge to leave. It made me think of the previous owner. "Do you think Samson, the old owner, was the last descendent of whoever wanted to keep the secret of the hoard?"

"A guardian would make sense."

All this chatter didn't accomplish the most important thing. "How do we open the door?"

At this, Ward frowned. "I'm not entirely sure we should."

"That's just the magic talking. We have to get inside. You said there's probably a treasure behind it."

"There most definitely is. However, it is important we proceed with caution lest we unleash a curse."

Funny he mentioned caution, given he'd yet to do anything like I'd seen on television. For one, he didn't cordon off the area or vacuum up the dust, nothing. Then again, I couldn't blame him for being eager for a peek and maybe skipping the usual protocols.

I recited one of the facts I knew about magic. "Spells require maintenance to stay active. And I'm pretty sure no one's been down here in a while."

"Some spells can remain dormant and powerful for a very long time." Sweat beaded his brow. "A possible curse isn't something we should dismiss."

My first impulse? Offer to bite the bullet if he was afraid. I mean, come on, dragon treasure! At the same time, I should maybe listen to a pro and not that urgent tug reminding me I had dynamite currently stored in a bomb-proof container painted with the name ACME. A joke gift from Mindy and Reiver at Christmas. A theme repeated in the Wile E Coyote sticker for the dent in the rear passenger panel of my car. Poor Tina. After the zombie incident, her cherry-red exterior suffered trauma from a cow.

But back to the door Ward wouldn't open. "Are

you saying we'll never be able to see what's on the other side?"

"Of course, we will; however, we also have to be cautious as to how we get there. We don't want to unleash anything nasty, especially since we have no idea what kind of magic a dragon is capable of."

"I thought the elves cast the spell." I gazed in confusion at the door.

"They cast the warning that is supposed to keep people away. However, what is inside could have been cursed by Satrina herself. It would explain why the elves and dwarves worked together to hide it."

He'd just laid out the perfect backstory to an epic quest where the intrepid farmer girl finds an ancient secret, battles to free it, and gets the man. "You say the sexiest things."

"Okay?" I'd totally confused the adorable Ward.

I reined it back a bit. "How are you going to figure out if there is a curse inside?"

"By triggering it."

I blinked. "I thought we were trying to avoid that."

"Avoid harm. We'll need shield amulets to protect us, plus a set of containment markers to prevent anything from escaping."

"You almost sound as if you've done this before."

He grinned. "Because I have. It's my—"

"Job. Fuck, that's cool. So that means you have firsthand experience with curses. You can get a shield that will stop any bad mojo?"

"I can, yes, but I can't guarantee the effectiveness as this is my first encounter with a possible dragon lair. Here's to hoping the protective magic has decayed with time and doesn't do anything but fizzle when we release it."

"What's the worst we can expect?" My morbid side had to know.

"Death. Pain. I once encountered a cursed place that flayed the skin of the living. Quite horrifying. As was the portal that opened onto Hell."

"You've seen Hell?" My eyes widened.

"Yes. And then shut that door permanently." He shuddered in remembrance.

"Do you think there's a portal to another dimension?" I eyed the carvings with excitement. Imagine finding Narnia or some other cool place.

"I don't know." He placed his hand on the stone. He was pale, but he didn't run.

"Let's find out. Who do we call for a magical shield?" I remained practical.

"For something this complex, we'll want a warlock."

The strongest of magic users—and annoyingly male. They also didn't come at just anyone's beck and call. "How much is that gonna cost? I hear they ain't cheap."

"We're not."

It took a second to filter the meaning. "You're a warlock?" I couldn't hide my incredulity. "But you don't wear a robe." A warlock trait. Witches, like my friend Mindy, tended to wear everyday normal garb. The druids liked flowy dresses, while the satanic covens often chose to live naked. But warlocks tended to be a snootier bunch. They wore long robes, sported beards, and often carried a staff. Mindy explained it as a prestige thing, which women smartly didn't ascribe to.

"Robes aren't exactly useful when climbing around in forgotten tunnels or slogging through marshes looking for ruins. I save mine for ceremonial occasions."

That made sense. "Well, then, Mr. Warlock, when are you giving us these shields so we can open the door?"

"Soon."

"Why soon?"

"Because I want to do a bit more research and prepare myself."

"How can I help?"

"By not letting anyone else down here."

"Let me guess, not even me."

He took my hands. "I would never even dream of asking you to leave. This is your discovery. And I am simply thankful I can be a part of it. Thank you so very much."

"Uh..." All the right words left me flustered. Especially since he leaned in and kissed me. A strange thing to do, and surprising. We'd just met, and honestly, I'd never been the type that caused men to lose their heads. Explain then the impromptu embrace that brought tingles to my lips and other places.

It didn't last long enough to suit me and didn't keep me warm all the way to the top. I huffed and puffed by the time we crested the stairs. Fuck sex. I needed a massage and a hot bath.

I managed not to stagger to the ATV but was tired enough I threw myself in the passenger seat and waved at him. "Why don't you drive?"

He did so, exceptionally well, with Jilly still choosing his lap over mine, and we arrived at the farm without mishap. As we prepared to part ways, I kept hoping for a repeat of the previous surprise kiss. Maybe even some groping. Instead, Ward left, promising he'd return soon as he could while petting my goat's head.

Jilly was bummed. So was I, although I perked up when, that evening, he sent me a weblink to read up on dragons with a note, *Will you be around tomorrow?*

I'd planned on making deliveries to Mindy's bakery and the restaurant I had a deal going with, but I fobbed those tasks off on my farmhands, preferring to stick around for Ward.

The next day, there was a brisk knock on my door. Expecting my dashing archeologist slash warlock, I didn't think but flung open the door, only to gasp at who stood on the other side.

"You." Without even thinking, I kicked, nailing the fucker standing on my threshold in the nuts.

# CHAPTER
# FIVE

I didn't hold back in my kick to the jewel sack of the guy standing in my doorway. In my defense, he deserved it.

As Axel Miller—a.k.a. my ex, a.k.a. the fucking jerk—folded from my well-placed blow, I spat, "Asshole." I'd been waiting a long time, more than twenty years, to vent. He'd hurt me badly, physically and emotionally.

Seeing him bent over in pain gave me some satisfaction, but not enough. I swung my fist as he struggled with the pain in his balls. I connected with his jaw, snapping his head.

The big bastard recovered more quickly than expected and caught my next swing. "Geezus fucking Christ, Annie. Would you stop acting like a psycho?" Axel snapped, maintaining a firm hold of my wrist.

"No, I will not stop." That fucker long ago lost the right to tell me anything. I kicked him in the shin.

He grimaced but didn't let go. "You're as violent as ever."

"Only with you. How dare you show your fucking face after what you did to me!" I yanked on my arm to no avail. Strong bastard.

"I did what was best at the time," he muttered.

"Best for you, asshole. I'd really hoped you'd died. Horribly. Some kind of genital disease that made your dick rot off and burn every time you peed."

"I get it, you're pissed—"

"Pissed?" I exclaimed. "Understatement of the fucking year. What did you expect when you came here?"

"I didn't want to come. I had no choice."

That raised my brows. "What's wrong, are you in some twelve-step program that requires asking forgiveness of those you fucked over?"

"I should have known this wouldn't work. I tried to tell them," he grumbled. "Should have sent someone else."

The oddity had me asking a suspicious, "Wait a

second, tell who? What are you talking about?" Because that didn't sound like a man who'd shown up to make amends.

"The Cryptid Authority ordered me to come."

The unexpected reply had my brows shooting up so far they almost escaped my head. "What the fuck does the CA have to do with anything?"

"I'm investigating an incident on their behalf."

"You work for the CA?" Well, color me surprised. When I dated Axel, he was more likely to be arrested by them. Remember me mentioning my thing for bad boys? Axel, born on the wrong side of town and prone to fighting, would be a prime example. At the time, though, he'd been the hottest thing in jeans. And as his girlfriend, he treated me like a princess until the day he dumped me.

"I'm what you might call a freelance agent for the CA."

"Well la-di-da for you. That doesn't explain why you've got the nerve to show your face."

"Like I said, I'm on a job for them."

"Oh no you aren't. Leave." I'd always told myself if I ever saw Axel again, I'd be able to remain cool. Wow. Was I ever fucking wrong. I shook inside and hoped it didn't show on the outside.

"Not before I've looked around your farm and

asked a few questions," he stated as if I had no choice.

Think again. "Like fuck you are."

"You can't say no. You know the law."

"Yup. And I'm fine obeying it." Most of the time. "But I am not dealing with you. Tell the CA to send someone else."

"Unfortunately, neither of us have a choice. I was deemed most suitable given my familiarity with the area."

I snorted. "Hardly familiar. How long you've been gone? Or should I say ran off like a coward after breaking up with me." He'd not just dumped me. He'd shown no regard to the fact I was attacked by his other girlfriend within minutes of his departure. Brutally savaged because of him. Put in a hospital, maimed, ruined for life.

Because.

Of.

Him.

"I had no choice." His pathetic reply.

Once more, my eyebrows almost took flight. "No choice?" I could barely contain my incredulity. I still remembered the whore at my door saying, *"Stay away from Axel. We're meant to be together."*

Dumb me, I said, *"Who exactly are you?"*

She spat, *"Name is Frenchie, bitch, and Axel is*

*mine.*" Pretty sure she had more to say, not that I remembered much when I woke in the hospital, almost dead from a lack of blood. Busted not only in body but spirit. Axel didn't check on me once. As a matter of fact, I never saw or heard from him again. I could only assume he'd gone off to be with his baby mama who chose to blame me for his cheating tendencies.

"There are things I can't explain."

I cut him off. "I really don't care what kind of weak excuse you have. I'm over it." Over him, or so I thought. Seeing him again made me remember the thrill of his presence. He'd changed, and not. He still wore jeans and big blacks boots only partially laced. A jean jacket over a black tee. His hair was as dark and thick as I remembered with only a few hints of gray. His face was where I spotted the most changes, squarer, the soft lines of youth hardened, creases in the once smooth skin, dark stubble along his jaw. Still so fucking handsome it hurt.

I kicked him again but only managed to nail his shin.

"Ouch. Fuck. What is wrong with you?" he growled.

"I hate you. What did you expect?"

His lips pressed into a thin line. "I'm sorry."

An apology that no longer cut it two decades

later. "Doubtful." I stepped back from the door and prepared to slam it shut. He shoved a foot in the opening.

"Annie, I—"

Whatever he would have said got cut off as a car drew up alongside his motorcycle.

Ward exited his vehicle. Being a shit, I shoved past Axel and pasted on my brightest smile as I exclaimed, "Ward, honey, I'm so glad you're here."

# CHAPTER
# SIX

Ward might have been initially surprised by my exuberance, but I'd give the man credit for catching on quick.

"Sorry I'm late. I got detained because I stopped to get you breakfast." He held up a bag of goodies from a bakery I knew well: Hexed Cupcakes. It was run by my BFF and had the best treats in town, thanks in part to me. I supplied her. Eggs, dairy, and other fresh produce, that is. Weed wasn't legal in my state. Yet. But I had plans for when it happened.

I snatched the bag. "Delicious choice. Let's eat inside."

I ignored Axel and walked back into my house, assuming Ward followed, only to have my uninvited guest growl, "Who is this?"

Before I could make up a lie, Ward did it for me.

He stuck out his hand. "Howard Cunningham. Archeologist for the Cryptid Historical Society and good friend of Annie's." He winked at me, and his lips curved in a way that gave me flutters.

*Take that, Axel.* Was it petty that I enjoyed Axel's scowl?

"Axel Miller. Field agent, Cryptid Authority."

"And what brings a CA investigator to Annie's farm?" Ward asked, moving close enough to wrap an arm around me. A nice possessive touch that I knew Axel noticed.

"It's classified CA business."

"I certainly hope you haven't lost track of another necromancer," Ward taunted. A jab that I appreciated. After all, the CA dropped the ball last year when my town became the victim of a dark plot. Too many people died, got zombified, and then died again before the necromancer was stopped. Ahem, I helped by the way.

Rather than reply to the accusation, Axel had a question of his own. "What interest does the CHS have in Annie's farm?"

"Who says he's here for the farm?" I tilted my head at Ward and managed a vacuous smile. "I missed you."

"I missed you more," Ward murmured without missing a beat.

Someone coughed.

I held in a smirk as I said, "Felt like forever but for a good cause. Your fault I worked up such an appetite." The less-than-subtle lie hit Axel hard. I could tell by the way his nostrils flared. Did he remember how bad I got the munchies after sex? He should, since he always drove me to the nearest drive-thru before I got too hangry.

"Your breakfast will have to wait," Axel snarled. "Annie and I have business."

"No, we don't. Whatever you're looking for, I hope you don't find it and you get fired for being shit at your job." His meek apology would never make up for what happened to me.

"Annie..." Axel interjected a note of warning that I chose to ignore.

"That's Ms. Jenner to you. Buh-bye. Do let the door hit you on the way out." I didn't pretend to be nice. It wasn't in me.

Ward wisely didn't comment until we heard the hum of Axle's motorcycle receding. Then he eyed me over a fresh scone and a cup of coffee that I poured with hands that shook—why I couldn't have said.

"Care to explain what that was about?"

I wanted to say no, but that would be giving Axel too much power. So I offered the basic outline. Ex-boyfriend. Dumped me out of the blue then had his other girlfriend come over and beat the shit out of me, putting me in the hospital with partial amnesia. I skipped the part where I almost died and lost my ability to ever have kids of my own.

The bit he heard raised his brows. "Wow. That's intense."

"No shit."

"Sounds like that ex of yours is a piece of work. But in good news, at least you escaped a lifetime with him."

"I did." No need to mention the scars left behind. I sounded pathetic enough already. I changed the subject. "So, are you ready to do your warlock thing?"

He grabbed my hands. "I'm ready if you are."

"Fuck yes. Do me. It. The door. I mean." And then I shut up because he kissed me.

# CHAPTER
# SEVEN

It was a nice kiss. Sweet. Soft. Interrupted.

*Gaa.*

Jilly came trotting from deeper inside the house, four hooves clattering on the floor as she barreled for Ward and slammed into him. That head with its single, stabby horn wedged its way between us, proving an effective form of sex control, not birth. I didn't have to worry about that. Hadn't for a long time. Sad face.

"Your timing is shit, Jilly," I muttered as Ward stroked her floppy ears.

"Actually, it's probably a good thing, as we should conduct our business before pleasure."

"I don't know if I'd call opening a mysterious door business, entirely." Because honestly, the idea of discovering treasure excited me.

The statement widened his grin. "On that we can agree. Shall we?"

He automatically took the ATV backseat with Jilly in his lap, his satchel once more strapped to the front. I doubt Axel would have ever agreed to ride bitch. He had surplus testosterone. Hated the fact I was so strong and independent. Was always trying to hover over me. Do things for me. Lift things and stuff.

Sigh. He was so hot that way.

But unhealthy. So very, very bad for me. A man like Ward would be much better. Bringing me breakfast. Respecting me as a woman.

I took a gentler route to reach the cleared field and the staircase, yet despite the easy ride, Ward's hand came to rest on the curve where my hip flowed into waist. It made me hyper aware of him. When we stopped, Jilly bounced off, but he remained a moment, sliding forward and nuzzling my ear to whisper hotly, "Thanks."

A grind of his lower body at my backside had me sucking in a breath, and then he was gone, checking out the wrong hole. I glanced down at my disappointed crotch.

*Soon.* Because if Ward didn't do something about the fire he ignited, I'd put it out myself. I had a nightstand drawer with all the tools I needed. Hopefully it wouldn't come to that. I'd prefer flesh to plastic.

I joined Ward at the top of the staircase. He rummaged in his satchel, pulling out pouches and a candle.

"For the protective spells, I assume?" I hovered with interest.

"Correct. For them to work, I'll have to anoint you."

"Go ahead and get me wet." I meant it as dirty as that sounded.

Did he take advantage?

Nope. He drew on my forehead with a finger dipped in oil and then ash. My skin tingled as he traced, but that was it. The only consternation came when Jilly decided to investigate and sneezed in the pot of dust he used to paint. Her exhalation sprayed it into a cloud, which she then inhaled, leading to her sneezing and wheezing while bucking her tiny hooves.

Silly goat. I giggled, feeling light as a cloud. "I feel fluffy."

"Completely normal. Relax with it. Allow yourself to float."

A part of me thought this might be a bad idea given all the stairs and my tendency to be clumsy at inopportune moments. A deep breath made that worry go away. I closed my eyes and exhaled, releasing all my tension.

*Aaaaah...*

I almost fell asleep as Ward hummed and chanted, a low and repetitive sound. I swayed and then snapped awake as he took my hand, leading me down the stairs. When had we started our journey?

"We go?" Two tiny words that emerged slurred. Everything in me moved sluggishly. Part of the shield I imagined.

"It's time to open the door."

"Protected?" I asked, knowing this was important.

"We have everything we need," he assured.

As if I even needed that. I could hear music, wordless but melodic, drawing me deeper underground. I floated down the steps, weightless as a cloud. When we reached the door with its giant eye, I wanted to touch it.

So I hugged it, my cheek against the stone. My hands splayed, palms flat. Cold. So cold and vibrating. The slight hum changed in pitch, intensifying. The rock I leaned against brightened, as if it lit from within. I closed my eyes and basked in the light and sound. Reminded me of that night so many decades ago. This was where it originated from.

The grinding noise startled me but not as much as the stone under my cheek moving. I reeled back to watch as the door slid aside, the brilliant light beyond blinding and sending me to my knees. An arm over my eyes barely helped, and I wished I could cover my ears as the music crashed into me. Slammed me with the purest of notes.

When the last one stopped its lingering vibration, I opened my eyes and screamed at the giant orb staring back at me.

## CHAPTER
# EIGHT

I YODELED, AND YET IT DID NOTHING TO REMOVE THE gigantic eyeball staring at me. Unblinking. The pupil vertical.

*"Annie, wake up."*

The voice insisted and managed to break through my panic.

A dream.

A nightmare. This was something I could control. Wake up. Just open my eyes and—

I saw nothing, only darkness. Nothing. A crushing oblivion—

I sat up with a gasp. *Where am I?*

It took a moment to realize I sat on lumpy ground and that the sky outside gleamed with bright stars and a half moon. Better than a giant eyeball.

A concerned visage leaned over me. Ward with his brow creased. "Annie, finally. You're awake. Are you okay?"

"What happened?" Other than the fact something had crawled into my mouth and died. I wanted to hack and spit at the dry, metallic taste in my mouth.

"You got impatient. The minute the door opened you went inside. I didn't have a chance to assess or disarm any traps. Soon as you trespassed, you triggered a spell. Whatever it was hit you hard, and you passed out."

"Oops." I remembered nothing other than the giant eye. Which wasn't real. Nothing had an eyeball that big.

"How do you feel?" He helped me sit up.

"Confused. How did I get here?" Because if I'd passed out below...

"I carried you."

Well, that was unexpected. "Thanks. That's a lot of stairs."

His grin turned rueful as he said, "I'm sure my legs won't thank me in the morning."

No shit. Still impressive he'd managed it. "Sorry I fainted on you. What did I miss? What was on the other side?"

"Nothing."

"What?" I blurted out.

"I'm sure at one time a treasure did exist, but we must not have been the first inside. The room was stripped clean."

"But you said there was a spell protecting it. It knocked me on my ass."

"You did trigger a spell, but not necessarily the original."

I poked a hole in his theory. "Why curse an empty room?"

"Perhaps the thief wanted to hide their actions and replaced the spell to foil discovery."

"So no treasure? That sucks." My lips turned down.

"Agreed."

"I want to see the lair." I went to rise, only to waver on my feet.

"I think you should rest first. That spell lashed into you pretty hard."

"I guess a little nap wouldn't hurt since there's nothing to see." The words soured on my tongue. I'd had such great hopes.

As we headed for the ATV, I glanced around. "Where's Jilly?"

"When we emerged from underground, she fled in the direction of the farm."

"Poor thing. Must have been scared." I'd probably find her hiding under the covers in my bed.

"She certainly can move fast when she wants," he said, grabbing me when I tripped and nearly fell face first.

"You should see her when she knows the pizza guy is coming up the driveway."

I didn't argue as he helped me into the passenger seat of the ATV. I slumped against his back for the whole ride home, completely exhausted. I should call Mindy for one of her special cupcakes.

Instead, Ward lifted me from the back of the ATV and carried me to bed.

I managed a mumbled, "My hero," before I fell asleep.

I woke alone.

## CHAPTER NINE

Ward had put me to bed fully dressed and departed. He hadn't laid a hand on me. Nor copped a leer at my defenseless body. Instead, he left a note.

*Hope you enjoyed a good rest. I'll be back tonight with dinner.*

Sweet. Especially considering he'd seen me snore and drool. My best friend assured me it wasn't pretty, but I'd been holding off getting one of those sleep machines. I wasn't even forty yet, dammit. I didn't want to mimic Darth Vader in my sleep. Not until I'd locked down Mr. Right.

Pushing back my covers, I stretched, surprised by how well I felt. After the exhaustion caused by the blasted remnants of the spell, I'd expected stiff limbs at least.

I bounced out of bed wearing entirely too many

clothes. The band on my bra left a deep line in my skin that had only partially eased by the time I got out of a ridiculously hot shower.

It occurred to me, as I dried off, that I'd yet to see Jilly. Beyond odd and straight onto concerning.

"Fluff butt, where are you?" I crooned as I dragged on my robe and headed downstairs.

The farmhouse had two floors with the second being an attic converted into a master bedroom with angled bath. The peaked roof made it so the whole thing required a short person to use it. Like me. It amused me to imagine Ward trying to bend over to use the shower. Maybe he'd agree to try out the clawfoot bath instead. I'd scrub his back—and other dirty parts.

I hit the main floor with no sign of Jilly and a realization I'd completely dropped the ball on the whole farmer thing. Here it was—I glanced to check—eleven o'clock the next day and I'd just gotten up. What of my chores? The animals? Free-grazing herds still required care.

A good thing I'd hired people to help out. I'd been transitioning to a more managerial role. Still, that didn't mean I could shirk my duties, especially now that I knew I didn't have a dragon's treasure hoard on my property worth gajillions.

I went about my work, checking in on the barns

and paddocks, even the garden, which spanned over an acre now and thrived with Mindy's special help. At harvest we'd hire some teens to pick the vegetables and fruit, the wage being only one of the perks. I fed them, too, and sent them home with extras for their families.

I spent a few hours making the rounds without a sighting of Jilly. Odd because a few of my staff mentioned seeing her around. Apparently, someone had dressed her in a purple romper I didn't remember buying and certainly never put Jilly in. So who messed with my goat?

Could it have been Ward? Jilly did seem to like him.

*Vrrrrm.* I whirled at the distant sound, glancing over the paddock and barren field to the trees lining the driveway. Wind must be flowing in the right direction for me to hear that far. A motorcycle by the sounds of it.

Axel? I hated the hopeful way my mind said it.

It better not be him. I had absolutely no interest in talking to Axel. Seeing him revived that moment of betrayal when he'd dumped me, simply saying, "We can't be together. We're not the same." It hurt. Up until that point, I'd never realized he saw us as different. Thought the color of my skin didn't matter to him.

But that wasn't the most hurtful thing he did. The worst betrayal was the woman at my door, a hand on her slightly rounded belly, smirking as she claimed to carry his child. Ordering me to butt out.

I remembered seeing red. The jealousy morphing into extreme pain. It hurt so much. And not just emotionally. I woke with stitches holding my middle together. Part of my intestine gone. My womb? Also a victim.

I was lucky to be alive, the doctor said. Everyone declared it as if I should count my blessings. It was a nightmare. I'd lost everything in one fell swoop.

Because of Axel.

As hatred and the psychic wounds from the past split open, my hand clenched around the screwdriver tucked in my belt. Not as good as a knife when it came to stabbing. Maybe I should use the hammer and bash his head.

My fingers dropped to my side. Killing Axel would send me to jail, and he'd win. I had to be cooler than him. I pretended he wasn't there. Let him get tired of waiting and leave.

I stayed in the paddock, fixing the loose sections, tying them in place with metal wire that wound through holes. I kept my back to the house even when the prickling at my neck became unbearable.

Eventually Axel drawled, "How long you going to pretend I'm not here?"

Fuck me for being obvious. "Until you go away," I snapped.

"You're being childish."

The use of the word "child" had me seething, and I couldn't help but grip my hammer. "What do you want, Axel?"

"I told you before, I'm here on behalf of the Cryptid Authority. I'm investigating an incident."

"I'm sure you are."

"This is serious, button."

"Don't call me that!" It was a nickname I'd not heard since he last used it. His term of endearment being shorthand for cute as a button. The dumbest thing ever but, at the time, I thought it adorable.

"When did you get to be so irritable?"

I had a dry response for that. "You bring out the best in me."

"Since that's the case, then I'll do my best to avoid you while I conduct my investigation."

The arrogance stunned. "I haven't given you permission."

"I don't need it given my mandate with the CA."

"This is my land. My people. My place. You don't belong. And I don't want you here." I stood toe to toe with him, which meant me angling as high as my short ass could go, but he leaned down to close the gap, putting us nose to nose.

"I'm aware. I live with that decision every day."

What did it mean? Rather than ask, I focused on his supposed reason for being here. "What exactly are you investigating?"

"We received a report about lights in the sky and singing."

I snorted. "Sounds like a party to me."

"Do you know what I'm talking about?"

"Nope."

"Are you sure? Because it apparently happened again last night."

"Then I missed it. I was in bed early."

"With your boyfriend?" His lips curled, and I could have sworn I smelled a spark of jealousy.

"None of your business." Primly spoken, and slightly gleeful. I wanted it to bother him. Let regret eat his insides the way it pulverized mine for so long.

"If he was here, then I need to ask him if he saw or heard anything."

"Why does the Cryptid Authority care about lights and music anyway?" I couldn't quell my curiosity. Especially since I knew exactly what he spoke of. Only what I'd seen happened decades ago. He indicated something more recent.

"I'm not at liberty to say."

That caused a scowl. "No info and I'm supposed to just cooperate?"

"Yup."

"And if I say no?"

He stared at me, the brown of his eyes more golden flecked than I remembered. "There was a time you would have never said no to me."

"Yeah. There was, and then you fucked me over."

"If I'd known what a clusterfuck it would cause, I would have never started things with you."

That hurt. I gaped at him. "What is wrong with you?"

"Nothing. The problem is you." He turned from me, and for a second, I couldn't breathe. How dare he!

I shoved him hard enough he fell, barely missing a cow patty.

Pity.

He bounced to his feet with a low, "Don't push me, button."

"Or what? You'll dump me? Been there, done that. Ended up in the hospital." My rapid-fire retort saw him recoiling.

"I thought if I broke things off, you'd be safe."

He didn't even deny it was his fault. "You knew I was in danger? Knew and never told me?"

"I did as I was told. Ended things with you. It wasn't enough."

Did he expect me to feel bad because his other girlfriend had jealousy issues? "Your actions got me hurt. and I never even had a chance to defend myself because I didn't know it was coming."

He ducked his head, his lips pulled taut. "For that I'm sorry. I never wanted anything bad to happen to you."

"And yet I'm the one who paid the price for your fuckup. I hope it was worth it." I let all my bitterness spill into that statement.

His lips turned down. "No. But given who my father was, I never had any choice."

Head held high, I stepped past him. "There's always a choice. You just took the easiest one."

I wanted that to be my parting shot. Only I forgot about the cow poop.

My boot hit the mush and slid. I didn't go down alone. I grabbed onto Axel and took him with me.

Should have known my plan to use him to break my fall would fail. Somehow, I ended up on my back, under Axel.

"Get off me." I heaved at him.

"Not until you listen."

"Going to whine some more about how you weren't man enough to say no to temptation? How you really loved me, and it was just an unfortunate turn of affairs?"

"There was no temptation. And I did love you."

He dared to claim that after all he'd done?

I shoved at his unbudging frame. "You're such a jerk. Why won't you just go away?"

"I did already, only it didn't work. I never forgot you, button."

A sweet lie was still a lie. "Well, you leaving worked for me. You did me a favor, actually. I'm a successful farmer now."

"So I noted, but are you happy?" A question posed with an intensity that had me almost squirming under him.

Why even ask? It wasn't as if he cared. I wanted to declare myself ecstatic with life, but I feared he'd see right thought it and guess how lonely it could be at night when it was just me in the house. "My happiness is none of your business."

"I wanted you to have a good life, button. I thought I was giving you that."

"Wow, did you ever miss the mark. Now, if you're done, get off me."

"Button, I—"

Axel never did finish that sentence on account he suddenly went flying.

## CHAPTER
# TEN

Lying on my back on the grass, I gaped in surprise as Ward stood there, arms crossed, glowering. Not at me, but Axel.

"What the fuck?" Axel recovered quickly and popped into an aggressive stance, the kind that screamed, *Put up your dukes.*

"It's called showing you how to respect a woman."

"Who says I wasn't?" Axel snapped.

"Because I heard Annie tell you to get off." Ward didn't back down despite Axel's glower.

"We were talking."

"Sounded more like you were bothering her," Ward retorted.

My head bobbed at the verbal tennis match. Over me. Kind of hot.

"How about you mind your fucking business?" A ruddy color filled Axel's cheeks, an indication his temper flared.

"It is my business when it concerns her." Ward pointed at me. I didn't get a cheap thrill at his protective possession, which surprised. After all, I loved it in the movies when dudes got all alpha with their ladies.

"Annie and I have history."

"An unpleasant one by the looks of it." Ward knelt to offer me a hand. "Are you okay?"

I let him help me rise and nodded. "I'm fine. I didn't need your help, though." I had things kind of under control.

"Sorry. I couldn't help myself coming to the rescue."

Axel uttered a disparaging noise. "Fucking gag me. We all know Annie wasn't in any danger. We were simply talking."

"Your idea of talking is a lot like being held prisoner," I retorted.

"I think it's time you leave." Ward tucked me to his side as he made the demand. Kind of ballsy, and yet I understood he tried to help. So rather than elbow him in the jewels, I allowed it. Maybe Axel would listen to another man since, apparently, he was hard of hearing when I spoke. I didn't want him around confusing me. I hated him, and yet remained attracted. What was wrong with me?

The guy had cheated on me. Impregnated another woman who then almost killed me. And when I would have pressed charges, both disappeared. Until now. Which reminded me.

"Where is Frenchie?" The name of Axel's side piece who hurt me so badly.

"How the fuck should I know?"

"Are you seriously that big of a jerk?" She'd carried his child. Surely he'd not lost track. The Axel I knew would never abandon his kid. Then again, it turned out I'd never really known him at all. He'd definitely been a liar and lacking in integrity. "Way to take responsibility."

"I have. I know what happened in the past is one hundred percent my fault."

"Good for you. I don't care. Now go away." I glanced at Ward. "Let me go get cleaned up so we can do have that dinner we planned."

"You get ready. I'll ensure he leaves."

"I have official business here."

"Really? Where's your warrant?" Ward riposted. "Until you have one, you're not welcome."

Technically, I should be the one tossing people

off my farm, but I'd had enough of Axel. It took everything in me to walk away and not look back. A battle lost when I reached the house, only to see the two men facing off in the distance. What were they saying to each other? Would they whip out their dicks and spray each other with pee, trying to make a claim?

And who did I want to emerge victorious? Because it should have been obvious.

The whole situation left me feeling confused, which wasn't something I enjoyed. By the time I changed and returned downstairs, only Ward waited for me on the porch. No motorcycle or its rider. The pang had nothing to do with disappointment. It was anxious relief.

"What did he want?" Ward asked.

"To annoy me, which I am determined to not allow," I declared.

"Good for you." Ward glanced around. "I'm surprised your goat isn't rampaging to greet me."

So was I. "She's been around, but she's lying low today." Weird. Kind of like this entire week.

"You ready to go?" Ward asked with a healthy dose of uncertainty after perusing me head to toe.

I take it he wasn't a fan of my outfit. I wore a tie-dyed T-shirt dress in shades of purple and pink, bright green clogs, and a bead-fringed shawl. An ensemble that only cost me eighteen dollars and ninety-five cents at a yard sale. I knew how to bargain shop. My name brand underwear cost me pennies because of Santa's mug on the ass. So what if I wore it out of season?

Ward took me to dinner at an Italian place, very dark, with secluded booths for privacy—or to hide me? He sat across from me, a perfect gentleman who didn't once try to play footsies. Discouragement had me sighing into my wine and drinking too much of it when he also neglected to try to feel me up under the tablecloth. We didn't share a spaghetti that ended in a kiss. Instead, I drank a lot of wine. Three glasses to be exact. Enough to be tipsy and amorous. After the meal, he drove me back to the farm. We'd no sooner parked in my driveway than I was climbing Ward and kissing him.

He allowed it for only a second before groaning, "I can't."

I wiggled in his lap. "I beg to differ."

"You've been drinking."

"Hardly." Just enough for a glow.

But he'd apparently been programmed by the feminist police because he said, "I'm sorry, but we can't. You are not in complete control."

Yes, I was. But Ward continued to respect me.

I wanted to cry as he left me horny and alone. Joke was on him, though.

I didn't need him for an orgasm. The more shocking thing, when I rode my pink vibrating rocket to orgasm, it wasn't his face I saw when I came.

# CHAPTER
# ELEVEN

I woke the next day to Jilly in bed with me. No idea where she'd been or how she'd gotten into her green plaid jumper and tied a bow around her horn. All I cared was I could snuggle the warm little body, and she uttered a happy noise in her sleep.

Pancakes with honey for breakfast had my Jilly bouncing, but what surprised was her sudden interest in a bowl of milk to drink. Usually, she liked sugary crap. But today when I went for the creamy fresh stuff, she insisted on copying me.

Look at us maturing and making healthy choices.

Having woken at my normal time, I did a quick round of the farm, checking on the status of stuff. Had everything running well enough I treated myself to a trip out to the empty dragon lair.

Jilly rode behind me sedately, sitting like a proper goat, her ears not flopping about or her tongue lolling as usual. We got to the hole, and my stomach fluttered. I stood at the opening and, for the first time in my life, understood the term cold feet.

I didn't want to go down there. Not one bit. Especially not alone. What if something happened to me? What if I encountered another spell, only this time I had no Ward to rescue me?

Fear wasn't a familiar emotion for me, and neither was caution, yet they led to me turning away and saying, "I'm in the mood for popcorn and a sappy movie. What do you say?"

"*Baaah.*" Jilly agreed and then uttered a noise that had me shaking my head.

"We are not watching *Wallace & Gromit: The Curse of the Were-Rabbit.*" Jilly's favorite movie indulged in on rainy days when she chose to abandon my side for the dryness of the indoors.

"*Blergh.*" My goat was less than impressed I wouldn't cave to her demands.

"I have a better idea in mind." Maybe the antics of a certain groundhog in a classic with Bill Murray would take my mind off things.

We left the field with the staircase, but the shiver it gave me didn't disappear even when I snuggled under a blanket. I really meant to stay awake to enjoy the best part of the war between man and rodent, only my comfy couch and the oversized glass of wine put me right out.

And I dreamt.

*The stairs were the most illuminated I'd seen them, each step distinct and dust free. I held the hem of my skirt because, for some reason, I'd chosen to go traipsing in a dress while wearing fine slippers. Golden with hints of silver, just like the many varied bangles on my wrist. Odd, because I owned very little jewelry, my flashing LED skull necklace being my pride and joy, along with my dangling wreath earrings.*

*The hum vibrating from my lips didn't echo, not in this place. I didn't give the song words, just a melodic shape.*

*At the bottom of the stairs, a familiar door awaited, the eye ringed in strokes like lashes. I stopped singing and waited. Unlike previous occasions, it opened without any touch, sliding silently to the side in invitation.*

*No hesitation fumbled my step as I marched my ass right in. I had to admit to being curious and wondered what I'd see. I recalled nothing of my first visit with Ward. The spell hit me hard and took my memories. Was this my mind's way of showing me what happened?*

*I shielded my eyes as if I expected a bright light. It took a few paces before I realized I didn't need to cover them. I'd entered a massive chamber, surely bigger than possible given the rules of gravity and structure. It appeared the world followed different rules here because the ceiling curved so high overhead I couldn't see it, nor did there appear to be any kind of columns for support despite the fact the walls of the massive chamber were made from hewn giant stone blocks like the ones used to build the pyramids. How did they get here? Who built this place? Dragons had short arms, and none of the stories ever mentioned them doing masonry.*

*But then again, what did I really know of dragons? They'd been extinct for a thousand years at least.*

*As I went to step deeper into the cavernous chamber, I noted the floor underfoot appeared to be polished obsidian. I could see my reflection in it, but one I didn't recognize. My hair, rather than forming a wild curly halo, had been tamed into braids that coiled atop my head and were threaded with gold and silver strands. A circlet of the same twining color rested upon my brow. Rather than my usual comfortable, if eclectic garb, I had on a gown of pale yellow cinched below my boobs which almost spilled out of the dress given how low they'd cut the neckline. I looked like a princess. More shocking, I didn't actually hate it.*

*My glittery two-toned slippers peeked from the ruffled hem as I walked and glanced around. I saw no sign of treasure. Nor dragon. Not even any bones. Also, not a hint of dust. An empty tomb. How disappointing and exactly what Ward had described.*

*I made it to the center, where a golden disc, lined in silver, proved to be the only color in an otherwise seamless floor. My fingers traced the disk etched with the same eye as I'd seen on the door.*

*The mark of Satrina.*

*I didn't say the name, and yet it echoed around me, startling me enough that I abruptly rose.*

Satrina. Satrina. Satrina.

*The noise buffeted and pushed against me, getting louder and louder. I took a step back, my foot pressing down on the disk.*

Click.

*The round plate sank. I immediately jumped off. Maybe nothing would happen.*

Whir. *My eyes widened as the hole peeled open, and from it rose a pedestal with a covered bowl on it, radiating a cold so intense I shivered.*

*A voice boomed from behind.* "Begone!"

*That sounded like—*

*Before I could even think of Samson's name, the blast from a shotgun had me squeaking and ducking behind the pedestal I'd accidentally called forth. A peek over the edge around the round bowl atop it showed a young version of Samson—younger even than the one I'd met in a driveway late one night—dressed in medieval garb.*

*"You shouldn't be here!" He lifted his gun, about to take aim again.*

*"Me! What are you doing inside my dream?"*

*"You're somewhere you don't belong, girlie."*

*"Actually, I do belong because I own the land with the dragon lair."* And while I wasn't sure how deep the law said I owned, I could lay claim to the entrance and stairs.

*"You shouldn't have come. The danger is too great."*

*"You mean the curse? Because too late. I got some of the backlash."* I grimaced. *"Unpleasant, but I survived."* Not to mention, I'd gone through much worse.

*"Back away from the pedestal,"* he ordered.

I shook my head. *"Like fuck am I making it easier for you to shoot me."*

*"I'll shoot you if you don't."*

*"Now listen here..."* In my agitation, I nudged the bowl on the pedestal, and it wobbled.

*"No."* Samson breathed the word.

*"Why?"* I tried to right a wrong, but the bowl slipped out of my hands, falling from the pedestal and hitting the floor hard enough it cracked into several pieces.

Samson leaned close and squinted. *"Where is it?"*

*"Where's what?"*

He turned a widening gaze on me. *"What have you done?*

He said it like an accusation. A normal response?

*Defend myself. "I have done nothing wrong." I dared anyone who found a cool hole in the ground to not check it out. Seriously. Only an absolute boring-ass coward would have not wanted to have a look inside. The only person who got stung was me. And I felt fine now.*

"It's not too late. Devote yourself to a lifetime of purity and perhaps it can be averted."

"Purity is not my thing. I can't go two sentences without saying fuck. I can't fucking help myself. See? It's a real fucking problem."

"The purity I speak of is of the flesh. Abstinence is the only way."

*I laughed much too hard at that.* "As if I'll give up sex. In this day and age, it's my body, my choice. If I want dick, I'm getting dick. Real dick. Plastic. Might even have a girl wielding it. I'm at an age where I'm keeping my options open."

"Better a woman than the bearer of seed."

*My nose wrinkled.* "Way to make dick sound like the worse choice."

"You mustn't allow it to be reborn."

"Fear not, ain't nothing getting born from this." *That ship sailed when Axel's baby mama sliced and diced me. The doctor's report said she used a tine-like weapon, sharpened like blades, as the four slashes were perfectly parallel, similar to an animal attack but on a larger scale.*

*"Heed my words,"* Samson proclaimed.

*"Heed mine. Find someone else's dreams to haunt."* *I'd thought I wanted weird in my life, only now, amidst it, I found myself enjoying it less than expected. Angst was a new thing for me.*

*"Stubborn twit,"* Samson mumbled, aiming his gun again. *"Should have taken care of you when I had a chance."*

*He fired.*

*I screamed.*

Only to find myself sitting up on the couch, the movie long over, Jilly snoring by my side, looking pudgy around the middle. Might need to put her on a diet.

Both of us could use it given my trackpants dug into my waist. I grimaced as I literally heaved myself off the sofa and to a real bed, where I didn't dream of weird old rooms underground and guys with shotguns.

It was worse. I got to relive the night Axel broke my heart.

# CHAPTER
# TWELVE

I woke in an understandably foul mood that worsened given it came with nausea and bloating. Add in the fact I somehow also craved food and I hated life.

Jilly remained abed, legs up in the air, snoring, her round belly making me frown. If I didn't know better, I'd wonder if she'd been frolicking with the males. Impossible. The vet I'd had checking on Jilly's health assured me she couldn't breed. Perhaps I should get a second opinion because she sure looked like a goat with a kid in the oven.

I headed downstairs and was in the kitchen prepping my coffee when the distant sound of a motorcycle had me grumbling. "Not again. Stubborn fucker."

This time, I didn't screw around. I grabbed my shotgun and headed for the front porch. I had it aimed by the time Axel pulled to a stop. No helmet to remove as he swung off the bike. As if Axel would ever mess up his luscious locks. It took a real man, like Ward, to think of safety and possible head injury.

Okay that wasn't a flattering comparison to Ward. It made me even more irritable as I snarled, "Go away."

"I'm here on official business, button. I need to talk to your staff."

"Tell the CA to send someone else."

"Don't make me apprehend you for obstruction of justice."

"I'd like to see you try."

Axel arched a brow. "Why, button, is this your way of making sure I put my hands on you?"

That accusation dropped my jaw. "Like fuck. I want you to leave."

"I don't think you mean that." He took a step then another.

"Fuck off." I steadied my shotgun, full of buckshot usually meant for scaring off the foxes and other critters that liked to go after my hens.

"You won't shoot me."

"Wow, you really are more stupid than I remember." It was my final muttered warning as he got closer.

Suddenly, Axel lunged. I fired. Above his head, damn him, because unlike the zombies, I wasn't the violent type against other people. When he got close enough, though, I swung the gun like a club. He caught it and wrenched it from my grasp.

That didn't stop me from fighting. I punched, kicked. Even slammed my head against his chin. It did nothing to save me from the plastic cuffs he slipped around my wrists.

I cursed him out the entire time he carried me inside and bound me to my own kitchen chair. "Cheating fucker. Lying asshole."

Only when he was done embarrassing me did he stand and coolly say, "I might be most of the things you claimed, but I never cheated on you."

"Liar!" I yelled as he walked out my kitchen back door. "I met your whore. Did you dump Frenchie and the baby like you dumped me?"

The words hung in the silence left behind with his departure. An absence that lasted all of ten seconds before he marched back in.

"What did you say?"

"Touched a nerve?" I taunted. "Does the truth hurt?"

"What truth? What are you talking about?"

"Your girlfriend, the pregnant one. As if you don't know I met her the night you dumped me. The night you were too cowardly to tell me the truth," I spat. "Frenchie told me all about the baby and you and how I was just a side piece before she went all psycho on me." Given my lack of memories after that point, I could only imagine I'd worried about hurting the infant as the reason why she'd been able to maim me so badly.

"Wait, is that why you asked about Frenchie? She told you we were a couple?" Incredulity marked his words.

"She outed you, fucker. Told me what a two-timing bastard you were."

"Fuck. Fuck. Fuck!" Axel yelled, raking a hand through his hair.

His agitation only increased my pleasure. "How many other girls have you lied to? How many bastards have you abandoned since?" I couldn't stop the stream of cruelty. I wanted to hurt him as badly as he'd hurt me.

"I see we have lots to talk about. Later. Once I've questioned your staff."

"There is nothing to talk about. Cheater."

He crouched in front of me. "I might be many things, button. A liar? Yes. An asshole? Yup. But I swear I never fucking laid a hand on Frenchie. And I have no children. None. On that you have my word."

"Your word means nothing," I shouted as he left. Explain that to the flutter in my chest when he said he'd never stepped out on me. Could Frenchie have lied? But why? What would she gain? Other than the hottest guy in town.

Still, even if he hadn't slept with her, it didn't negate the fact Axel had dumped me. Had to have heard about me being in hospital and never once visited. Never cared.

If only I could say the same.

It was weeks—okay, probably more like an hour—later before he returned to find me out of the chair, armed with a machete. Hopefully he would only bleed in the kitchen. Tile would be easier to clean than old wood floors. Then again, what was a little sanding and varnishing when I'd have the satisfaction of knowing Axel was dead.

He eyed me, the knife, and then ignored both to wash his hands and dry them. Asshole acted as if he had the upper hand.

When he was done, he leaned against the sink and stared at me. When he spoke, he didn't say what I expected. "Your farm is really well run."

"I know." The pleasure at his words annoyed. I didn't want compliments from *him*.

"Your staff all love you."

"Duh." I treated them well.

"None of them seem suspicious or as if they're hiding anything."

"I could have told you that." I'd hired from town and the surroundings, choosing people with a true love for the land and animals. But none of them lived on the farm. They were usually gone by seven. "Why does the CA even care about a light in the sky and some stupid music?"

"We got a tip it might be important."

"A tip from who?"

"A woman I trust. Yvonne."

Jealousy irrationally clawed. "What makes you think you can listen to this Yvonne?"

"The fact she is the most accurate seer on the cryptid crime prevention task force."

I arched a brow. "Maybe she had a bad day."

"Yvonne is never wrong. Which means I must have missed something. Who else lives around here?"

"No one close by. Not since I bought Samson's place."

"Anyone living there?"

"Nope." Then because I couldn't help myself, I offered a coy, "You never questioned me."

He slewed a glance my way. Arched a brow. "Are you saying you saw strange lights and heard some music?"

"No."

"No you didn't or no you won't tell me?"

I smirked. "Guess you'll never know."

"You should be careful, button. I don't know yet if what I'm looking for is dangerous."

"I'll be fine."

He snorted. "Maybe. Maybe not. You're too human, just like most of your staff."

A slag that had me bristling. "Says the other human in the room."

He glanced away, and it hit me suddenly. The way he said it, how he'd even been able to tell.

"Wait a second. Are you saying—"

He cut me off abruptly. "I haven't said a thing."

"Holy shit, you're a cryptid. That's why you dumped me. Not because of my skin color." It made so much more sense.

He gaped. "Why would you think I cared about that?"

"Because you never actually explained. You told me it would never work. We were too different. And then your baby mama shows up—"

"I never slept with her!"

"—and I'm thinking, fuck me, I was just a side piece."

"You were never just a side piece," he growled.

"No, merely an inconvenience when you suddenly discovered you belonged to the cryptid club. Expendable, which was why you cast me aside."

"That's not what happened!" he roared.

Like literally roared. I eyed him. "Lion?"

"Hell no."

I could think of another animal that he resembled. "Werewolf?"

"Yes," he hissed. "And before you ask, my sudden introduction to it at almost eighteen proved unexpected, given the Lycan gene usually appears in my family at a very young age."

"Wait, are you saying your whole family are wolves?" That raised my brows.

"Only on my father's side," he mumbled.

I blinked. "I thought your father left when you were like two."

"Yup, because, according to him, I obviously wasn't his son. A true son would have inherited the gene. Turned out I was just a late bloomer."

"How is it I'm just learning about this?" I flailed my hands.

"Because, like I said, I found out late in life. High

school senior year and it freaked me the fuck out. I kept it secret."

It explained the mood swings that started halfway through our dating. "Why didn't you tell me?"

"I couldn't."

That brought a frown. "Why not? It's not like it's a crime to be a werewolf." Not since the law passed in '93 that stopped the segregation of the wolf Packs from normal society.

"It's not a crime, but at the same time, it changed my life. With my change in status, I suddenly belonged to my father's Pack and was expected to follow some strict rules."

"Like don't pee on things that don't belong to you?" I made light because, inside, I reeled. I'd not expected this revelation.

"Actually, marking is encouraged."

This was juicy and confusing. "Well then, what didn't you like? Don't eat your neighbors? No bathing in fur after Labor Day? Flea collars by Easter?"

"I wasn't crazy about the rule that says the son of an Alpha can't date a human chick."

"One, I'm not a chick. Two, why not? Wasn't your mom human?"

"My mother was a mistake according to my father." His lips flattened.

"Ouch." A cruel thing to be told.

"It was uglier than that. The Pack is very much about bloodlines."

It hit me like a rake in the face after I stepped on it because my lazy ass forgot to put it away. "You dumped me because my genetics weren't good enough for you."

"You were perfect for me. It was my Pack that had a problem with our relationship."

"So you tell them to fuck off."

"I did, which was when I got warned to either break things off or you'd pay the price. Only they lied. I did as they said, and you got hurt anyhow."

"Wait a second, are you saying your werewolf pack sent Frenchie to attack me?"

"No, that was all Frenchie. She couldn't handle rejection and acted." He uttered a bitter laugh.

"Let me get this straight, because you wouldn't fuck her, she tried to gut me?" It wasn't any better.

"She meant to kill you." He looked at the floor rather than me as he whispered, "You weren't supposed to survive."

"I'm surprised she didn't come back to finish the job."

"She planned to, only I handled her before she could."

The way he said it... "What do you mean by handled?"

He stared me dead in the eye as he said, "I killed her for what she did, and I told my father that if anyone ever laid a fucking hand on you again, I'd come back and kill him, too."

## CHAPTER
# THIRTEEN

Some women might have fainted in shock. Gasped. Freaked the fuck out at hearing her ex-boyfriend killed someone and threatened his own father.

Me?

It took everything I had to restrain myself from throwing myself at him for a really tongue-filled kiss.

I reminded myself I still hated Axel, even as the story of our breakup took an unexpected twist.

Rather than embarrass myself, I clapped. "Bravo. Epic story. You almost had me believing it."

Axel frowned. "It's the truth."

"According to you. But excuse me if I call bullshit. You loved me so much you walked away. Loved me so much you didn't visit me in the hospital after I almost died. Loved me so much you never once fucking called, sent a postcard, nothing!" I was shouting by now.

"To keep you safe."

I jabbed him in the chest. "I *was* safe. When you were with me. But you left, and I was alone. Alone when that bitch attacked me. Alone when the doctors told me I'd never have kids because a psycho gutted me. Alone after my parents died in that crash. Alone when the drought hit and I was hand watering my crops. Alone every night because you lacked the balls to stay by my side." The rant expelled from me in increasing decibels until I heaved with exertion.

His jaw tightened. "I was trying to spare you."

"Bull shit."

"Fine, the truth was I couldn't face you. Couldn't face what I caused to happen to the person I loved most in the world. And I'm sorry for that. More than you could ever know."

"Blah. Blah. Blah." I made a talking gesture with my hand, and inside I simmered. My rage had taken a different turn but was still as intense. "The truth is, if you loved me, you wouldn't have left."

We might have argued some more about it, but Jilly chose that moment to canter into the kitchen and halted at the sight of Axel. Her nose twitched.

His did, too, which was admittedly weird to see.

"What the fuck is that?" he asked, pointing to my sweet goat.

"Jilly. My pet. Not a snack, in case your furry ass is thinking of taking a bite." That earned me a glare.

"What is she?"

"Pygmy goat."

"That's not a goat." He sounded quite certain.

"Yeah, she is, with a few messed-up chromosomes, as you can see by her horn."

"She doesn't smell right."

"You don't smell right," I chided as my goat sidled sideways to hide behind me. "She's delicate and sweet, and how dare you try and make her feel bad!"

"How long have you had her?"

"Long enough to know she's not the reason for your stupid lights in the sky."

"They're not stupid," he muttered. "Yvonne says—"

"Yvonne can kiss my ass." She could also kiss my fist. Did she see that in her future? Was it even possible to hit someone who could predict your every move?

"You're being childish."

"Actually, it's called bitchy. Stubborn with a hint of asshole. If you don't like it, leave."

His lips flattened. "Beginning to see why you remained single."

"I'm not single. How funny you blocked out my boyfriend from your mind."

"He's not your boyfriend."

"Excuse me? Why do you say that? You think I'm not good enough for a scholar?"

"I think you don't look like a couple."

"We most certainly are."

"Ha. Doubtful. How did you meet?"

"It was like something out of a romantic movie." I offered a simpering smile. "He showed up all sexy and Indiana Jones like, and well…how could I resist him? Ward is just so handsome and smart. Jilly and I absolutely adore him." I laid it on thick.

"What's his interest in you?"

"The fact I'm cute as a button." I used it against him.

Axel scowled. "That's not why he's really here."

I clucked my tongue. "Wow. Talk about throwing some shade. Is it so hard to believe a hunk like Ward would be interested in me?"

"Never said that. And you're avoiding explaining. How did you meet? Before you think of lying, keep in mind I can always call a buddy over at the Cryptid Historical Society."

"If you must know, I found something old on my property."

"Found what?"

"Ancient dragon lair." As his eyes widened, I explained. "But no actual dragon. Not anymore. Or even any treasure. Not that I knew that when I found the stairs. Good thing I called for help because the magic protecting the place knocked me on my ass even with Ward shielding me."

"Whoa. Hold on and back up. You found a dragon lair? Where?"

"None of your business. Ward told me not to let anyone close."

He didn't like that. "CA outranks CHS, so guess whose order counts more."

"Why do you care about some old dusty lair? It has nothing to do with your case," I lied. Fuck yeah, I lied.

Didn't matter. Axel wouldn't budge. "I'll be the judge of that. After all, no one knows where the light originated from. Maybe you triggered it when you found the cave."

I'd never admit he might be right. "I think you're mistaken."

"I still want to see."

"It's a long walk," I warned.

"I'll survive," he replied dryly.

As I headed outside, Jilly chose to stay behind rather than stumble at my heels. Odd how she didn't like Axel. Only showed she had good taste.

I straddled my ATV parked nearby, and when Axel asked, "Got a second ride?" had too much pleasure saying, "Nope, so either get on the back or walk."

He eyed me, the narrow seat behind, the implied emasculation, and growled, "Like fuck. I remember how you drive."

"Whatever." Then because I wanted to be a shit, added with all the innuendo I could manage, "Ward enjoys getting behind me."

The tic high on his cheekbone was new. As was his sudden decision to pull off his coat then his shirt as a reply.

I blinked at the wide expanse of muscle, and more muscle, and holy fuck that vee.

I averted my gaze. "What the hell, Axel?"

"If I'm going to keep up, then best I do it on four feet, not two."

Wait, did he imply—

Before I could truly process his words, the boots were kicked off and the pants removed. A naked Axel calmly stowed his shit on the passenger seat. Then he winked.

"Close your mouth, button, or you'll catch flies."

I'd apparently already caught a fever because I flushed head to foot at seeing him. Not the young sexy guy I knew as a young girl but a full-on seasoned stud with a full chest of hair and an endowment few could match.

Sue me, I looked. He noticed. He hardened and growled. Man growl, not beast.

I swallowed—my spit, not his cum—before saying, "I thought wolves only shifted on full moons."

"That's for the betas and lesser in the Pack. Alphas control it at will."

With that, he turned furry—a painful-looking process that changed a man whose body I'd once licked into a four-legged beast who could eat me, as in a meal, not a pleasurable snack.

The transformation complete, Axel shook out his fur and then eyed me.

It might have struck me as weird if I'd not fought zombies. Putting my ATV into gear, off we went.

# CHAPTER
# FOURTEEN

While I spent part of the trek gunning the engine and going too fast, somehow Axel—the wolf—kept up with me.

My mind whirled with everything that had happened in the last hour. From him not cheating on me—supposedly—or hating the color of my skin to finding out I never really knew Axel at all. I'd certainly never suspected he came from cryptid roots. His mom had been a tired-looking woman with a cigarette always dangling from her lips. Bitter with a chip on her shoulder. She'd died in a fire that swept through the trailer park she lived in not long after Axel left town.

As for Axel's dad, I'd never heard anything about the guy other than he was a bum who walked out on a little kid and his mom. It left me with so many questions and confusion.

Axel claimed he'd broken things off and left town to protect me. In his mind, he'd done the only thing he could. It made me wonder what would have happened if he'd chosen to stay, to fight for us. To fight for me. Apparently, he never loved me enough to even try, and if he thought I'd give him a second chance, he was out of his furry mind.

Never mind the fact he was sexy. And a were-wolf, which was also super sexy. I was not ready to forgive. Not even close.

We reached the field I'd cleared and the entrance down to the dragon's lair. I remained sitting on the ATV, hugging myself at a sudden chill. Once more, I had no interest in seeing what lay below. Weird. Maybe some form of PTSD from the magical blast I'd suffered.

The wolf, his dark fur streaked with silver, glanced at me sitting atop my ride. I could see the question in his gaze. "My legs are not in the mood today. You want to see, go right ahead. Straight down. You can't get lost."

Without further ado, he disappeared, and I sat, tapping the steering wheel for a second before craning to eye the pile of clothes at my back. Shirts, pants, boots, wallet. I snooped and found the expected cards: driver's license, credit card, a hundred bucks cash, and, tucked away in a slot, a worn picture of me.

My hand trembled as I held the old snapshot taken at a fair in one of those booths. Why had he kept it? I'd burned every last thing that reminded me of him.

Disturbed, I hastily shoved everything back and turned to face the hole in the ground.

How long had he been gone? Should I be worried? What if he got hurt?

Just as I thought about maybe going to check, the wolf appeared and then freaked me out as his strides in my direction went from four-legged canine to two-legged naked hunk.

I averted my head as Axel snared his clothes and began to dress.

"This field, it used to belong to Samson." More statement than query.

"Yeah. He died when the zombies got him, and I snatched up his place at auction." I briefly explained the stone mound I'd removed, uncovering the stairs.

"You've been down to the bottom?"

I nodded. "Three times. The first when I found it and then twice more with Ward." I didn't mention not recalling the last time.

"That explains your scent. I also smelled two others who passed through recently."

"Probably Jilly and Ward."

"Hmph." A grunt instead of a reply. "I am curious why you called it a dragon lair though. There's nothing at the bottom but a small room barely large enough for two people."

"It opens up when you go past the door."

"What door?" he asked sharply.

"The one that's not there anymore since Ward opened it. It slid into the wall. It blocked off the lair. Big thing etched with a giant eye fringed in lashes. Ward says it's the symbol for some dragon called Satrina who died a long time ago."

Axel kept staring at me. "There is no door or etched anything. Just stone blocks cemented together."

"Impossible. You must have not seen it somehow." Which made no sense. Once you reached the bottom, it was the only thing there.

"I see perfectly fine in the dark, and I'm telling you there's no door."

The moment he said dark, I blurted out, "It's because of the magic. Must be a spell or something hiding it from you."

He didn't dismiss my suggestion out of hand but appeared to mull it over. "Possible, I guess."

"Guess?" I couldn't help a lilt in my repetition. "I'm not lying about this. There was a door. And a room beyond. Not that I remember it 'cause I passed out. But Ward saw it."

"You have pictures?"

"No, but only because electronics don't work once you reach a certain point."

"You should stay out of there. Something ain't right about this place." The frown encompassed not just the hole in the ground but the entire field.

"You don't get to tell me what to do."

He glared. "I'm serious, button."

"My name is Annette. Or better yet, since you're here on official business, why don't you stick to Ms. Jenner."

"I will call you whatever I damn well like, *button*. Now, scooch your sweet ass so I can drive us back."

"My ride. I drive." I patted the seat behind me.

"I am not in the mood to play."

"Neither am I, so same choice as before. If you don't like it, then walk."

"Maybe I will." As he went to strip off his shirt for a second time, rather than carry his clothes for him, I suddenly hit the throttle and sped out of there. Petty, but I was all right with it. Although curiosity had me wondering if he'd have to carry his shit in his mouth.

An hour later, I almost went looking when I saw him striding back, fully dressed, a glower on his face.

Rather than annoy me some more, he straddled his bike and left without a word.

I'll admit, it miffed. I ate my sorrows in the form of a freshly made apple pie topped with hand-churned ice cream.

## CHAPTER
# FIFTEEN

Blame the bourbon I poured on my dessert before bed for my dream that night.

Once more, I found myself skipping down the stairs to the lair absolutely happy as a lark, no hint of exertion. In no time at all I arrived at the door with Satrina's symbol. It remained wide open, and I stepped inside to find the chamber empty. Samson didn't emerge to confront me, nor was there a backlash of magic.

A glance down at my frame showed I wore yet another ridiculous gold and silver outfit. Off the shoulder this time and empire style so it flowed from under my boobs. The sparkly polish on my toes made me want to get it done in real life. I could just imagine my BFF's shock if I asked her to come get a pedicure with me. I wasn't one to do the girly thing.

The strange emblem in the floor didn't click as I stood on it. Okay, I hopped. No pedestal came rising up. Boring. I kicked the stone underfoot and sighed.

Why bother dreaming if nothing interesting happened?

As if in answer, I heard the bubbling of water. Intrigued, I followed the sound to the back of the massive cavern and found a doorway tucked behind an arch. As I stepped inside, a wall of humidity hit me, and I encountered the source: a bubbling hot spring. Oh, hell yeah. I stripped faster than Randy that time I asked if he wanted to go skinny dipping.

In seconds, I was basking in that heated natural tub, eyes closed, relaxed, steaming like a lobster in need of some greasy buttering. Knowing Mindy, she'd have compared it to something gross and healthy like broccoli.

"Does my lady require anything?"

The deep voice startled.

"Ward?" I splashed water as I turned and used the side of the tub to hide my naked bits. I liked to choose when and where folks saw me nude.

Ward towered over the tub, but he wasn't the sweet guy I'd come to know. This version was hot as fuck. He was dressed in a loincloth and nothing else. Dream Ward was ripped. So many ridges I wanted to run my hands over. I tucked them behind my back, but I'd have sworn he read my thoughts with the way he smiled at me.

My dream was looking up. I loved a good sex dream, waking up with a quiver if done right.

I slid to the side and beckoned. "How about you join me?"

"As my lady commands."

I expected him to step into the tub. He did, but only after he dropped the loincloth.

My eyes widened. Well. No disappointment there.

He descended the carved stone steps, each one concealing more of him as the water rose No biggie. Soon my greedy hands would be grabbing that body and learning its shape.

I crooked a finger, and Ward began to sit, only to pause and then straighten.

"Something wrong?"

"I heard something." He craned to look behind.

"Don't be silly. There's—" It was then I felt it. A prickling of my senses, a coolness invading the heat.

"We are not alone. You might want to get dressed."

Suddenly getting into a tub without a towel to dry off didn't seem like a great idea as I rose from the heat to the rapidly chilling air.

"What is it?" I asked, scrambling for my useless

dress, which did nothing to combat the lowering temperature.

"My enemy doesn't want to see me with you," he mumbled as he turned to confront the darkness infiltrating the cave.

"Who's your enemy?" How many enemies could a historical society professor—Wait, was he a professor?—have?

"You know who. Do not play coy." A cryptic statement.

I could think of only one cockblocker. Axel. Invading not only my thoughts when awake but now my dreams, too. Asshole.

I wouldn't allow it. After all, this was my fantasy. If I wanted to fuck Ward in it while pretending I was some grand lady in an underground lair, then by the gods I didn't really believe in, I would.

I marched to the far side of the pool, where the icy darkness gathered, ready to give it a piece of my mind, when it coalesced into Samson, armed with a sword.

Unexpected. I'd honestly expected Axel. Maybe he didn't care who I slept with? But do you know who shouldn't care less? Samson. Yet there he stood.

"I told you to git!" he admonished.

"You git. You interrupted my sexy times, you ornery old bastard."

"You don't understand what you're doing. This honor is not for the unworthy."

I could have snorted. "Okay, this is obviously a joke dream, because I am more than worthy for any man." I didn't need validation. I had faith in myself.

"Your opinion is unwanted, guardian," Ward drawled.

"Foul creature, you should have never returned." Samson bent his knees and held out his blade.

"And you should know you can't stop me."

With a battle cry, Samson lunged, and I blinked as a sword flashed into view as Ward suddenly moved around me. Where did he find a sword?

A quick glance to my side showed he'd changed. No longer the naked Chippendale, he wore armor, the steel not reflecting light. The breast plate molded to his body, as did the bracers on his arms. He wore gloves and held a mace with ugly-looking spikes.

Fully dressed and yet super-hot.

Also, weird. My imagination was good, yet this went next level.

I backed away as the two men advanced on each other. A young Samson with his sword, lunging and parrying against Ward.

*Clang. Clang.* As they fought, I inched my way to the doorway out of the chamber. Forget having sex.

Even I had limits, and banging the victor—if it was Ward—as reward for killing Samson—who, while annoying, didn't merit being murdered—just didn't appeal.

Blame my earlier boredom complaint for turning my dream into a reality show Jerry-Springer-style.

I emerged into the main cavern, and the noise of the fight disappeared, yet the icy chill didn't. It followed, freezing the moisture on my skin, bringing a mighty shiver.

Fuck me, this wasn't fun anymore. I longed for my warm plaid jacket and Sherpa-lined BEARPAW boots. Hugging my upper body, I strode to the open doorway, only to halt as the edges began to waver as if something blocked its opening. An invisible force.

It didn't want me to go.

I didn't want to stay.

"This is just a dream," I chanted as I marched right for that shimmering spot. The chill intensified to the point my teeth chattered and my skin went numb. I forged ahead, one plodding step at a time.

"Do not leave!" Ward's command boomed, and I glanced over my shoulder to see him, a dark knight covered in a wet sheen of blood.

Sexy in the movies. In my dream? I didn't care for the tone or the look in his eyes. I wasn't some spoils that went to the victor.

"I'm going home." Never mind the fact my sleeping ass was already in bed. I wanted to wake up and exit this nightmare. I turned and began pushing against the force trying to keep me inside the lair. I gritted my teeth and strained, step after molasses-sucking step.

"You cannot depart yet. We have unfinished business."

The way he termed it brought a grimace. So much for lovemaking or tender, sweet nothings. Dream Ward was a jerk who could keep his big dick to himself.

If I could only move. Right at the threshold, I found myself frozen, unable to take another step. I grimaced and pushed to no avail.

"You cannot escape. Not until it's done."

"I'm not fucking you," I snapped.

"What you want is irrelevant." Fingers dug into my shoulder as he wrenched me to turn and face him.

I uttered a screech of annoyance. How dare he!

"Fight me. I like it. Submit and you'll like it, too."

"Not interested. Let go." I yanked against the grip he had on me. It didn't budge.

I dropped my body and swayed left and right, trying to loosen it.

He leered. "Then we do it the hard—"

My goat interrupted the threat as she came to the rescue.

Apparently, his armor didn't come with a cod piece. She nailed him in the nuts with her horn.

He let out a short scream, and that quick, he released me that he might clutch his groin.

"Good fluffy butt," I exclaimed as I grabbed her hefty body and ran. The barrier blocking me had disappeared. Didn't care, didn't stop to investigate. I bolted up the stairs, goat in my arms, huffing and puffing as Ward bellowed behind and under me.

"Come back!" He followed me up the stairs.

"Fuck you!" I gasped as I strained for breath. Where I found the strength to make the climb, I couldn't have said. All I knew was I could have cried when I saw stars ahead.

*Almost there.*

A triumph that turned into horror as a hand grabbed my ankle. I squeaked as I fell, losing my grip on Jilly. I hit the stone steps hard and got pulled down one before I thought to kick. I wrenched free as Ward came into view, his dark armor blending with the shadows, but his eyes...they glowed.

As did the hands he brought together.

Fuck me, I'd forgotten he was a warlock. As I prepared to be incinerated, I had time for one quick prayer. *Please don't let it hurt.*

Before Ward could complete the spell, a four-legged furry body leaped over me. A wolf.

Holy shit.

Axel.

He hit Ward, and I heard snarling and the creaking of armor. Not one to look a gift wolf in the mouth, I flipped onto my hands and knees before rising. I made it to the rim—freedom!—and only managed to run a few paces before my foot caught in a rut. I tripped. Whacked my head.

And woke in my bed, Jilly snuggled by my side, snoring softly.

Just a nightmare. Or so I thought until I saw my muddy feet.

# CHAPTER
# SIXTEEN

Waking up naked with mud on the feet and a sore tushy, as if I'd fallen for real and not in a dream ,led me to freaking out.

It didn't take much of an imagination to realize I'd been possessed. It was the only explanation. Someone had used my body as a puppet and taken me to the lair, where I almost had sex with Ward and was saved by Axel.

Hmm. Not as likely as me having simply wandered outside in my garden, hallucinating, probably because I picked the wrong mushroom to sauté for my dinner.

There were always aliens. Never knew when they'd mess with a human. The government was totally covering it up.

So many reasons why I could have been muddy, bruised, and naked in bed.

What happened to me? Faced with that question, I did what any smart girl does. I fled to have a chat with my best friend. I found Mindy in her shop, which opened at an ungodly hour even by farmer's terms. It should be noted I wasn't a before-dawn kind of country girl. My day required daylight to start. In winter, I paid someone to cover those dark early hours for me.

I entered the shop and inhaled deep. Instant contentment. I dared anyone to be grumpy when confronted with the scent of baking. Bread, muffins, cookies... My BFF and her fiancé—because Mindy and Reiver had gotten engaged—had expanded the original bakery so that Reiver, a former hunter for the Cryptid Authority, could have his own space to make yeasty confections that almost made me believe in God. His bread was just that good.

The moment I entered, Mindy saw me and jerked her head, a sign to get my ass out back. She left the counter in her new assistant's capable hands.

Martha had rosy cheeks and a rounded body. She looked like your sweet ol' grandma until she opened her mouth. Martha didn't put up with anyone's shit. I loved her. So did Mindy because after the whole zombie fiasco, where my BFF supplied folks with zombie-repelling baked goods, she had an increase in business, which led to a higher number of a-holes to deal with.

*"What do you mean you won't make a poison apple tart? I want you to treat me different right now because I demand it,"* punctuated by stamping and sulking.

Martha loved setting the demanding in their place. *"If you don't like it, then get your ass back out that door, or I will take you into the alley and teach you some manners."*

It should be noted no one knew exactly how Martha would impart those manners. No one dared to ask. One day, I would find out. When I wasn't busy dealing with dreams that were a little too real, an empty dragon lair that might not be empty, and an ex-boyfriend who came to my rescue in my dream against my not-quite boyfriend who—

I interrupted myself because, fuck me, this was complicated. I needed Mindy and her common sense.

As I headed into the rear kitchen, expanded since they knocked down the wall into the shop next door, the heat of the ovens hit me. A moment later so did a goblin.

Mungo landed on my shoulder and gave my ear a tug, chirping, "Friend."

Before you think Mungo was some cute and cuddly creature, let me set you straight. Scaly, green skin, beady yellow eyes, a nasty scar, and claws that could cause damage. But she smelled clean. Mindy wouldn't have allowed Mungo in the kitchen otherwise.

Good thing appearances didn't mean squat to me.

"Hey, green stuff. What's shaking?"

"Make a pie," Mungo stated quite proudly. At her pointing claw, I glanced at a lopsided monstrosity, filled with stuff I didn't want to get close to.

"Looks fantastic," I lied.

"Piece?"

Something moved under the crust, and I exclaimed, "What the actual fuck? Did you put beetles in there?" At Mungo's grin and rapid bob of her head, I shuddered. I had lines. Bugs was one of them.

"No share!" Mungo tittered before scampering down to stand proudly over her creation.

Mindy entered and smirked in my direction. "I can't believe you said no to the pie."

"Watching my bug intake." I patted my belly. My round pot belly. I really should stop hitting the ice cream at night.

"Does that go for fresh cinnamon rolls?" Mindy arched a brow. "I was just about to ice a batch."

As if on cue, her handsome partner entered, six foot something of sex on two legs. The man was seriously dreamy and totally in love with my best friend. Lucky bitch. They planned to get married at the summer solstice, and I was her lucky maid of honor. A good thing I had time to plot the most epic bachelorette party ever! With strippers, so many strippers. I wanted dongs to be flying around everywhere until my best friend just about died from embarrassment. She was so cute that way.

"Hey, Annie." The deep-voiced Reiver set down a tray of perfection, the rounded coils of dough hinting of the sugar and cinnamon inside.

"Hey, stud. How's it hanging?"

Without a beat, he replied, "Low and ready to swing into action." Nothing embarrassed the man, and it took a lot to get him to smile. Unless your name was Mindy. The man was soft where my BFF was concerned. "Everything all right at the farm?"

"Why do you ask? Did you hear something?" He might have retired from active duty with the CA, but he still had connections.

He frowned, but before he could speak, Mindy jumped in. "You look rattled. I'll bet it's about that cave you found."

The one I'd downplayed when I spoke to her previously. "Yes and no. And..." I halted, at a loss for words. Unusual for me.

"Start talking." Mindy sat down, and Reiver leaned on a counter. They listened as I blurted it all out, from my blowing up the rocks, to the passing out, to the sex dream that wasn't.

By the time I finished, I expected Reiver to snort and tell me I should do better drugs. Mindy would probably tell me to take a plant or two to fix my dreams.

Instead, he pushed away from the counter. "I'll get my gear."

"Wait, what?" I blinked as he left. "Where's he going?"

"To fetch his weapons. Don't worry, he won't be long. He keeps a spare set in the shop."

"Why is he getting weapons?" Not that I minded. I never went anywhere without a few options. My truck parked outside, for example, held an axe, a revolver locked in the glovebox, and a can of bear spray. I'd had to stop toting around my fertilizer sprayer filled with gas after it leaked and almost caught my truck on fire. Who knew the fuel would chew through my rubber washers so easily?

"It sounds as if you've got a cryptid problem," Mindy stated as she took off her apron.

"Me?" I couldn't help but sound surprised. After all, I'd spent my life hoping for some wild adventure and almost got it with the averted zombie apocalypse. I'd practically trained my whole life to be ready when the big battle came. But my current problem? "I don't know what you think we're going to fight. I haven't seen any monsters or anything."

"Meaning they're good at subterfuge."

"What makes you think it's a cryptid?" I asked.

"Because you don't seem like yourself." A soft assertion by the one person who knew me best.

"I'm fine." Not entirely a lie. Other than a bit tired, physically, I was fine. Just a little bloated. And constipated. Also hungry quite a bit. I really hoped I'd dreamed that three a.m. run to the kitchen where I stuffed my face with olives and ate spoonfuls of jam.

"Annie, have you seen yourself in a mirror?"

"I don't need to see myself to love myself."

"You don't look healthy." Mindy reached for my hands. Hot to my cold. It took her touch to realize the chill within me.

"Are you dissing my outfit?" I had no idea what I'd dressed in. I just kind of threw some stuff on and left the house. I glanced down at my T-shirt with its giant red fruit and the words Wanna Taste My Cherry? It had gotten a lot tighter since the last time

I put it on. "I might have gained a few pounds. Can you blame me? Axel is back in town."

"Another reason why we should come out to the farm. How do you even know he's telling the truth about working for the CA?"

"Um." Because he said so sounded dumb. I hadn't asked him for proof. But why lie?

"I want to see this field with the lair. Maybe the plants in the area can tell me a bit more about the history of the place." My BFF had an affinity for Earth, as in growing things. She took the term green thumb to a whole new magical level.

"Ward didn't want me showing it to anyone."

Mindy gaped at me. "Since when do you listen to authority?"

Good point. "Not sure what you think you'll see. The place is empty."

"Then no harm in us looking."

The fact I wanted to argue against her coming out to the farm was what clamped my lips. I was acting uncharacteristically. Even I could see it. I loved a good conspiracy. Loved poking my nose in places I had no business even more. Break and enter? Skirt a law? So long as I didn't get caught, I was always game.

Until now.

Now my palms sweated as I drove back to the

farm, followed by Mindy on the back of Reiver's bike. Mungo kept me company in the front seat. By company, I meant she slept and occasionally farted. Bug-pie farts stank in case you were wondering.

Once we got to the farm, I loaned Mindy and Reiver the ATV while I trundled along with the tractor. By the time I parked, Mindy stood at the end of the cleared field. Reiver watched, gun in one hand, long dagger in the other.

"Did you see something?" I asked as I passed by his tense body, Jilly at my heels.

"This place doesn't feel right," he said grimly.

I glanced around, the sunshine hitting the dirt and hunks of rock, the moss now exposed, dry and yellow. "If you say so." I would have loved to have gotten a tingle. Anything.

I went to stand by Mindy on the edge of my new field. It stuck out in a clear and perfect circle, the ground inside it freshly tilled.

"The entrance to the lair is in the middle." I pointed.

"I am not going in there." Mindy hugged herself.

"It's perfectly safe."

"I highly doubt that," Mindy muttered.

"What's got you all freaked out? There's nothing here." I stepped over the invisible line. "See? Fine?"

"Get out of there, Annie."

"I thought you wanted to see the lair."

"I can't." Mindy took a step away, arms still wrapped around her upper body.

"What about Reiver? Is he gonna chicken out, too?" I teased because her reaction freaked me out.

"He is not going anywhere near that hole without some protection. And neither should you. There is something really wrong with this place."

I might have argued, only the ground suddenly erupted with barbed vines that wrapped around my ankles and toppled me!

# CHAPTER
# SEVENTEEN

I hit the ground and felt myself being dragged. What the fuck? The one time I didn't have a bloody axe and, of course, living vines with deadly thorns burst from the ground to try and kill us.

I sat up and reached for the pocketknife I'd tucked away, along with a flashlight in my pocket. I used the six-inch blade and stabbed the vine, which contracted.

Ha, it could feel pain. I hacked and sawed at it. It parted enough I could pull myself free.

More of the writhing limbs snaked for Mindy, who held out her hands and prayed to the Earth goddess. Reiver stood by her side, gun put away in favor of matching daggers. He danced amidst the wriggling masses, slashing and stabbing.

Mindy hit the ground, palms flat to it, glowing

green as her goddess answered her prayer and filled her with magic. The voice that emerged from Mindy boomed and didn't belong to her. "Perversion of nature. Begone!"

With that simple warning, Mindy lunged for the vines, wrapping a hand around one long enough to draw whatever animated it. A brownish tinge edged her green magic.

The vine went limp in her grip and, when she dropped it, hit the ground and remained there. All of the plant limbs she touched lost whatever power animated them.

It was cool to watch, but I remained a little jealous. It would be nice if, for once, I could be the hero. Petty of me, I know, which was why I overcompensated with my clapping when my friend saved the day and cleared my field of the malevolence possessing it.

"That's it, bestie. You tell that weed who's boss!"

"That wasn't a weed." Mindy kicked the dead vine.

"Stay there," Reiver ordered as he strode to the middle of the field and surveyed the hole in the ground. His hands still gripped his blades.

I approached more cautiously. Part of it was remembering my previous hesitation but also my dream. No way had I walked all the way here and back in my sleep.

The stone edging around the stairs appeared old and worn, unlike my recollection.

"When was the last time you went down?" Reiver asked.

My mouth opened, and I almost said last night. "More than a day, why?"

"Looks like the tunnel caved in. You're lucky it didn't happen while you were down there."

"Wait, that can't be right. Those walls were solid."

"It only takes weakening the right spot." Reiver shrugged. "Whatever happened, there's no getting down there without an excavation crew."

I stared at the jumbled rocks blocking the stairs, unsure of how I felt about that. I'd have expected relief. Instead, nothing. The greatest find of my life taken away and nada.

Just how badly was I bespelled? And who was doing the magic?

A certain warlock came in mind and soured my mood.

We returned to the farm, me quiet and pensive, the lovey-dovey couple doing a piss-poor job of trying to ignore each other. As if I didn't catch the glances, the hand holding. Ugh.

We arrived to find Jilly and Mungo gone and the secret of who had been dressing Jilly solved, or so I assumed given the discarded romper on the floor and the bag from a tailor on the floor. The pair had bonded upon their first meeting. As per previous occasions, they'd chosen to go off on their own little adventures. A goat and a goblin. It was an odd match that worked because neither cared about their differences. Like me and Mindy.

My BFF canoodling with her man while I remained single.

"Bitch, stop making googly eyes at your fiancé and concentrate on dinner. You're in charge of dessert. Reiver, make us a carb that I can butter. I've got steaks for us meat eaters, brussels sprouts for the wanna-be bunny"—I eyed my vegetarian friend—"and rice."

It was my plan to have a wonderful dinner with friends. Hopefully, get past my obsession with the lair now that it was gone and get a good night's sleep.

The latter ran into a problem, given my best friend, who'd chosen to spend the night, moaned from the other room and I could easily imagine why. Since I wasn't about to cock-block her, I went for a walk.

A wolf in man's clothing joined me.

## CHAPTER
# EIGHTEEN

"You know for someone who was traumatized by being attacked, you take an awful lot of chances."

I gave Axel a side-eye. "Never said I was traumatized."

"You are, and it's justified."

I rolled my eyes. "Don't tell me how to feel."

"How about I tell you to stay away from danger instead, then. What the fuck, button?"

I didn't correct him on my name. "What are you complaining about now? And why do you care? You seem to have forgotten that what I do isn't any of your business."

He grabbed me, not hard but enough to spin me. "It is when you put yourself in harm's way. What would have happened if I'd not been around when that fucker went after you?"

I blinked at him. "You mean it really happened? Ward actually attacked me?"

"You don't remember?" Axel frowned. "Did you bang your head and forget?"

"Thought it was a dream, actually."

"A dream?" he shouted. "You're lucky I was staking out that field."

Rather than thank him, my lips flattened. "Why were you there?"

"Something's not right about that place. I wanted to keep an eye on it at night. I don't know how I missed your arrival. I never even knew you were down there until I heard you on the stairs."

"I thought it was a dream," I repeated.

"What happened?"

"I was in the lair again, having a soak in some kind of hot mineral pool, when Ward appeared and started saying some strange stuff."

"Like?"

I wasn't about to repeat the fact he'd called me his lady. "Just crazy shit. And he killed Samson's ghost. I think. I saw blood, which is impossible since Samson is already dead."

"Why did Ward attack you?"

"Why does any guy decide to rape a woman?" A dry reply that had me hugging myself. A part of me still felt kind of molested given my actions had been totally manipulated. What if I'd not escaped? I shuddered to think what might have happened. "Thanks for saving me. What did you do to him?"

His jaw tensed. "Not much. He used some of his magic and got away."

"Oh." Could he hear the disappointment in that one syllable? Now I'd have to worry about being ensorcelled again.

"That prick won't escape me for long. I expect he'll come around soon because of his interest in the lair."

"Don't be so sure. The stairs collapsed."

"Since when?"

I shrugged. "Since a few hours ago. I took a peek down, and they were just rubble."

"What were you thinking, going there after what happened?" His incredulity emerged a touch loudly.

"I thought I dreamed it all. And I didn't go alone. Good thing, too. Mindy took care of the killer vines, and Reiver was ready to decimate anything else that moved."

"And who is Reiver?" It was a low queried growl.

"Mindy's fiancé. No need to be jealous," I said in jest.

"I'll be jealous if I want to."

Not the answer I expected. "Saving me was nice

of you, but don't think that forgives you for what you did. We are not getting back together."

"Not yet."

"Not ever. Not after what you did."

"I will find a way to atone."

I almost lashed out because he couldn't ever fix the fact I couldn't have kids. At the same time, the attack by Frenchie wasn't entirely his fault. Could I blame him for the actions of another?

"You hurt me." A soft admission that I could make in the dark so long as I didn't look him in the eye.

"I did. And I hurt myself. I denied myself a chance to be happy with you." His fingers brushed down my cheek. "I regret that every hour of every day."

My skin tingled at his touch. "Pretty words. I'm not the same gullible idiot you knew as a teen."

"You were never dumb."

"I was when it came to you." It killed me to realize that the same sensual magic that enraptured me before had me under his spell again. I saw Axel, and despite everything that happened, all I wanted was...him.

"That's because we were meant to be together." His soft reply.

"Ha. You wish."

"I know."

"Know what, that you're feeling nostalgic? Get over it. I'm not interested in you."

"Liar."

"You're not that hot." The real lie.

"Prove it. Kiss me."

"As if I'd kiss you." A soft huff of words almost against his lips.

"You know you want to."

"Conceited much?"

"No, more like I know because we're meant to be together. I've hungered for you, button. Tried to tell myself it can't be as good as I remember. But no one ever compared."

Jealousy flared for a second as he admitted to being with others. So had I. Which was why I understood what he said. Sinead O'Connor sang it well when she crooned "Nothing Compares 2U."

But like he said, surely it couldn't be as good as we recalled. We'd had decades to build it up into something more epic that it was. We were young. Impressionable. Sex back then was new and always fun. More mature now, I doubted it would be as passionate.

Only one way to find out.

I grabbed him by the hair and yanked him close

enough to mash my mouth to his. The tingle exploded as all my senses ignited at once.

He didn't hesitate. His arms came around me, his lips caressed mine, and he joined me in the frantic kiss.

It was frenzied and hot. His tongue on mine a shivering delight. We were outside in the open, under the stars. No bed, no blanket, nothing but the short, mowed grass and the clothes we shed in our haste.

His body atop mine proved a heavy pleasure. My legs spread that he might lie between them grinding, his cock long, hot, and ready, pressing between our bodies.

Between my thighs, I pulsed, wanting him, any part of him, touching me. He had his fingers threaded through my hair as he held me close, the embrace never ending. My leg curled around his haunches as I arched into him, silently begging for more.

Rather than shift his hips to give me his shaft, he slid down my body, nestling between my legs, his tongue lashing at my nether lips and my clit.

My hips bucked, so he held me down and licked me until I came. On his lips, his tongue.

And then his body covered mine while I still

hummed from my orgasm. The tip of him pushed, and he whispered, "I want you, button."

For how long?" I didn't realize I'd spoke aloud until he replied.

"Forever."

The one word that melted me.

He slid into me, and I gasped, my nails digging into his back as he stroked me. Pushed and retreated in and out of me, bringing me to the brink and, each time, clenching me tighter and tighter. He had the shape and size to hit me in the spot, until I shattered again, coming so hard I floated out of my body.

I drifted back to my quivering flesh and found Axel breathing as hard as me. Good to know I still could give him a good workout.

"It's better than I recall," he murmured, kissing my neck, my ear.

"Mmm. Maybe. I might need a second round to be sure," I challenged. Later I'd regret my actions. Maybe. Or maybe I'd finally admit to myself that I had never stopped loving Axel.

He rose to it—literally—this time with me sitting on his lap in reverse so he could play with my clit while he filled me. I came hard, clamping down on his dick with my pussy while he nipped at my shoulder as he shuddered and came.

Little was said as we dressed. I think neither of

us wanted to ruin the moment. Only as we parted in my backyard did he draw me close to whisper, "I will see you tomorrow."

Rather than sound needy and ask him what time, I said, "Bring bacon."

His laughter warmed me all the way to bed. I was glad I didn't run into Mindy or Reiver. They would have asked about the stupid grin on my face. And I don't know what I would have replied. Good sex didn't mean I'd forgiven Axel or wanted him back.

Except I kind of did.

Being with him reminded me of the passion we used to share. Only with him. No one else ever came close. If he spoke the truth, he'd not cheated on me and had his reasons for acting as he did.

But I remained miffed he'd left. It was a hard pill to swallow.

It took me forever to fall asleep. I hoped to get a few hours' sleep before Minever—or should I call them Reindy—woke up early and had a morning round of sex.

I managed to sleep until seven.

On my way to get eggs for breakfast, really hoping someone would show with bacon, I was kidnapped.

# CHAPTER
## NINETEEN

I woke up in an impossible place. The dragon's lair. I must be dreaming because the path to it had been destroyed. Pretty sure no one managed to bring in heavy machinery to clear those stairs without me noticing, not to mention my situation had a bit of a supervillain vibe to it.

For example, I sat in a chair wide enough that the rope tying my legs to the spindles spread them. My arms were similarly tethered to the sides. The icing on the dream situation? I wore a thin gown, the type that you could see my nipples right through, short enough it rode up on my lap, exposing my legs. Judging by the breeze kissing my cooch? No underwear.

A sexy and heart-pounding look and situation when it happened to that chick in *Temple of Doom*. A little more ominous when it happened to me. I wasn't the damsel-in-distress type.

What the fuck had happened?

Last thing I remembered, I'd exited the chicken coop with my haul of eggs, slightly bent to get through the short door. My mind was somewhere more pleasant—and naked with Axel—when *bam*.

Nothing until I woke here. Only was I really here? I couldn't be sure anymore.

"The vessel awakens."

A turn of my head showed Ward stood to the side, once more decked out in full armor, sword sheathed by his side. Handsome, though his expression was cold.

Did he know I'd slept with Axel? Perhaps my subconscious felt a smidgen of guilt, hence why he appeared so cold. Still, jealousy was no excuse.

"What do you want? Why have you trussed me like a turkey?"

"Turkey is apt given my plan to do some basting. Or should I say stuffing?" Spoken with a leer.

"Like fuck you are." I pulled at the rope binding me.

"Please do struggle. It will make it more enjoyable for me." He slowly walked toward me, peeling off his gloves and tossing them to the side. I recognized the move, meant to terrify me. Cow me into submission. As if that would work.

"You know, needing to scare a woman to have sex is an indication of erectile dysfunction. There's a pill for that." I taunted because I didn't know what else to do. There appeared to be no slack in the rope holding me in place. Maybe I could goad him into slapping me hard enough the chair would tilt, hit the floor, smash, whereupon I would be freed and have a handy chair spindle as a weapon.

He didn't cooperate with my plan. "Insults, the façade to give the illusion of bravery."

"Not an illusion. I'm not afraid of you." I would fight to my last breath. It would just be easier if I had my hands and feet free to do it. Even better if I had my machete.

"What will you do, talk me to death?" Ward mocked, unbuckling his chest plate to set it aside.

"I will bite anything that comes close." I gnashed my teeth.

He chuckled. "As if I don't have a spell to protect against harm." He unbuttoned his shirt and untucked it from his pants.

"Why now? I mean, let's be honest, had you asked me to do the horizontal tango a few days ago, I'd have been naked faster than you could say Annie."

"This is a momentous occasion. It required preparation." The upper half of his body peeked as he peeled his shirt, and I began to worry. Where was a wolf when I needed one? Or a ghost with a gun?

My rescue came in the form of a goblin.

"No move," Mungo whispered.

I knew better than to look and give away my unlikely helper. How had Mungo found me? Was there another path into Satrina's lair? Obviously or I wouldn't be here. A way in meant a way out. If I could get free.

Unfortunately, the goblin's actions didn't go unnoticed.

"Your rescuer is woefully unprepared," Ward mocked.

I glanced down and could have groaned as I grasped what he meant. The goblin had the courage to help but lacked the right tools. Her butter knife wasn't making any headway on the rope tethering me.

"Goblins, such pesky critters. But useful with the right spell. I'll deal with you later." Ward waved his hand, and Mungo suddenly floated as if contained in a bubble. She pounded and opened her mouth to no avail. No sound. No escape. She drifted away toward the ceiling of the massive cavern.

"Where were we? Ah, yes. The next part of the

plan." Ward unbuckled the belt holding his sheathed sword.

"Why not say it like it is? You're planning to rape me because you're a little man with a little dick."

His lips quirked. "We know neither of those is true. And you're looking at this wrong. What is about to happen is a ritual, a needed one to bring them back."

"Bring who?"

"Take a wild guess."

"Um, hate to break it to you, but Satrina is dead, and I'm pretty sure no one has the magic to resurrect dry old bones." Even a necromancer could only do so much with a dead body.

"Our mighty queen might have perished, but before she did, she planned for the future and left us an heir. An heir lost until you discovered her last hidden lair and most precious hoard."

"Back up a second. You said this place was empty." An obvious lie in retrospect. Blame my hormones at the time for wanting to believe him. Also refer back to the fact I made bad choices when it came to men.

"Empty of the kind of treasure most expect. But in its place, something more precious. A trove of eggs."

"How many is a trove?" A dumb question but I

honestly had no idea. Was it more or less than a dozen?

"Enough that we can bring them back."

"By them, you mean dragons." His insanity began to make a crude sense. But for one thing. "These eggs have to be ancient. There's no way you can get them to hatch. Wasn't Serafina the last of her kind? Who would have fertilized them?"

"Interesting thing about dragons, did you know they're all female? A confusing bit of knowledge until you find out they can utilize any sperm to start conception. Human, animal, doesn't really matter. It's the egg that's important. Second to that, finding the right kind of vessel. One with enough remnants of the ancient bloodline for it to work. Then, they must be womb free, for the hormones of pregnancy are toxic to dragon ovum."

The more he spoke, the more my stomach clenched. "Wait, when you say vessel, are you saying you put the eggs inside something?"

"Someone." He held my gaze, and my throat constricted.

I glanced down at my rounded belly. "You put a dragon egg inside me?" I screeched. On the one hand, holy fuck. On the other hand, even bigger holy fuck.

"Your implantation went well. The ovum

appears to be adapting in size, indicating a meshing with the vessel. The next step is to inseminate it." Judging by the way he began unbuckling his pants, he planned to provide the latter.

"I don't think so."

"As if you have a choice. Do you know how long I've been working toward this goal? I made it my life's work to find this lair and bring back the rightful rulers of this world."

"Why? What do you get out of it?"

"Power. Wealth. I shall be the highest amongst humans when they return."

"You're insane. Dragons are, were, killers."

"The strong will always eat the weak. And the world needs that more than ever."

"Samson will stop you." I glanced around, hoping to see the ornery ghost come to life in this place. After all, he'd been insistent on my staying away. He'd come to my rescue the last time I found myself here with Ward.

"The guardian has been taken care of. The curse that kept them in this place was finally broken when I sundered his soul."

That sounded massively unpleasant. I stalled for time by blabbing. "How did you manage to work for the Historical Cryptid Society without them catching on to the fact you have a hard-on for dragons?"

"Everyone has their passion. Mine was for an extinct species." The top button on his pants came undone as he stepped in front of me. "I've been waiting for this moment my entire life."

"Do you hear how crazy you sound? Shoving old eggs inside a body, planning to fuck it as if you've got magical jizz that will bring it to life. Hate to break it to you, but you don't. It won't work."

"It will. Satrina left clues before choosing her final resting place. Preserved her legacy with magic. Even set in motion the acts that led to you being the perfect vessel."

"Wait, are you saying she was behind Frenchie's attack?" At this point, not much would surprise me.

"I'd say it would be a huge coincidence if she wasn't seeing as how you're perfect for our purpose. And I will be the one to bring Satrina's plan to fruition." He crouched, making him slightly lower than me in my seat. I wondered why until he pushed my light dress up even further, exposing me fully.

"What do you think will happen if you bring dragons back?" I asked in all seriousness.

"The rightful order."

"That includes you at the head of it."

"Yes. But at the same time, while I will be elevated above all others, humanity will serve and be protected." He pulled a tube of lube from somewhere and held it over my cooch. The fucker came prepared.

"Protected from what? Humanity is doing fine."

"We could be something better. The days when we served, we enjoyed the highest standard of living. No one was hungry. Or unclothed. Everyone had a home."

"If it was so great, then why did humans exterminate the dragons?"

"Because the dragons were misunderstood."

"Pretty sure it had to do with them eating us!" I pointed out.

"Meat is meat. And it isn't as if humanity suffered for losing a few here and there."

"Tell that to their families."

"Emotions. A failing the dragons do not suffer from."

"You really drank the dragon Kool-Aid, didn't you?" This conversation highlighted the pointless nature of arguing with a cult. They just wouldn't see any other opinion than their own.

"You act as if humans are better than other animals. Why?" he questioned, his head tilting to the side.

"Because we think. We feel. We create stuff."

"So do dragons. And like humans, they eat meat."

I wanted to claim it was different, only, in a sense, it really wasn't. As a farmer, I probably understood that better than most.

I wouldn't be able to change his mind, but I did have a question. "This egg you implanted. How do we get it out?" Never mind how he'd gotten it inside me. I hated to think what might have been done to my body when I was knocked unconscious that first time coming to the cave.

"Once inseminated, it must then be allowed to incubate at an elevated temperature—hot baths and saunas aid in that respect—until it has matured enough to be expelled."

"Expelled how?" I asked.

"The same way it went in." His gaze went to my cooch, and it involuntarily clenched.

"So you admit to molesting me and implanting a dragon egg without my permission!"

"I did. And I would do even more to ensure the return of the dragons. You should thank me for the honor I am bestowing upon you."

"Honor?" I snorted. "You need to work on your sales pitch." And I needed to get the thing in my belly out. Should I hit the hospital or a vet? Maybe if I squatted and pushed?

"Enough talk. Time to get cracking." He had the nerve to wink at his very poor joke.

The situation was dire. He shifted to his knees, and I realized the chair was the right height for him. I struggled to no avail.

This was going to happen. Fuck me, no don't fuck me. God fucking dammit. I wanted to fight. I cursed and yelled as he whipped out his dick.

My rescue came in the shape of a chunky goat, head down, stubby horn out. She speared Ward in the ass.

# CHAPTER TWENTY

My joy at seeing Jilly was short-lived.

Ward hadn't been joking about having a shield against harm. Poor Jilly went from about to tear him a new arsehole to bouncing off some kind of electrical field. The shock of it flung her tiny body across the room and left behind a smell of singed hair. Jilly hit the ground and didn't move.

"Fluff butt!" I reached for my pet without thinking and snapped the restraint on my left arm.

That widened Ward's eyes.

Hell, it shot mine open, too. I glanced at my other hand, still bound even as I tugged. For a second, I thought I had super strength. Nope. Still just Annie. The farmer. The idiot with bad taste in men. Now the incubator.

*Please don't let the thing inside me claw its way out of my belly.*

"Where were we?" Ward drawled, turning back to me.

"You were going to let me go?" I injected a hopeful lilt. Maybe I suddenly had the power of persuasion.

"Do you want me to chase you down before I overpower you? That does sound rather exciting."

"Perv." And to think I'd lusted after him. I hated how he spoke as if my being overpowered was a foregone conclusion. How insulting. If I bolted, and he chased, he'd find himself with a fight on his hands because I would find something to clobber him with. A plan that hinged on him releasing me first. This whole having me tied was unsporting.

"You obviously don't read much romance. My understanding is the bodice rippers women enjoy feature a male who isn't afraid to take what he wants, even if it's by force."

"Shows how little you know. We like a man who isn't a coward. Tying me up? Definitely makes you a big fucking pussy. What's wrong? Is the big bad warlock afraid I'll hurt him?" I taunted. After all, it worked in the movies.

To my surprise, it also worked in real life. "I fear no one, especially not a human like you."

"Then prove it."

"Very well." He pulled a knife and sawed the ropes around my legs. Then those on my remaining arm. I remained seated, barely breathing, wondering what game he played.

When done slicing through my tethers, he stood but remained close enough to tower over me. Perhaps he thought himself sexy with his shirt unbuttoned and draped on either side, the top of his pants undone. Two days ago, I'd have mauled his body. Hell, even now I couldn't deny he was handsome. Maybe I should try seduction. I'd faked interest with way worse. But there was something about giving in to Ward, about pretending, that turned my stomach.

He couldn't be allowed to win. And if running gave me a chance, I'd take it and maybe find a way out of this mess.

"You going to give me a head start?" I asked as he kept staring, the gleam in his eyes not as unsettling as the bulge in his groin area.

"I'll do better than that. I'm going to give you a weapon." He pressed his knife tip against my breastbone and lightly dragged it down, enough I feared he'd slice the thin fabric and flesh. He left the blade in my lap.

Grab it fast and lunge? Ignore it in case it was a trick? I wavered on what to do.

Ward retreated a step. "Shall I start counting? Let's say to one hundred. Is that enough time?"

His cockiness grated, especially since I had no idea how to get out of this cave if the main stairs were gone. Obviously, another exit existed. Where, though?

Perhaps, instead of a panicked escape, which involved me running pell-mell through dark stone hallways—that never ended well in horror movies—I should fight him right here and now. After all, he'd armed me with a knife.

Against a warlock.

Where was a flame thrower when you needed one?

Fuck me. Like seriously, fuck me if I didn't get away from Ward. I refused to be his monster baby mama!

I needed to stall a little longer to figure out a direction. "Are you counting Mississippi style or as fast as you can?"

"Counting too quick would ruin the sport," he replied indignantly.

As he feigned insult, I glanced around, remembering the pillar hiding the door to the hot spring. A dream or had it really happened? What if all the pillars covered an exit? It might explain how he got me here. There could be several entrances. After all, I'd never truly explored. What if I was wrong, though? Or chose the wrong pillar? Here was hoping Lady Luck was watching over my gamble—and made up for all those scratch-and-win tickets I'd lost on over the years.

"Do you want to count down and yell go, or should I just run when ready?"

"Let's go for the element of surprise." The sick fuck didn't even bother to hide his excitement.

Which led to me muttering, "I am so going to kill you."

My words didn't disarm him at all given he crooned, "I can't wait to feel you struggling beneath me as you receive my seed."

I shuddered but managed to get out of the chair to my feet.

Then contrary to what he'd said, he whispered, "One, two, three, and off she goes!"

My feet moved, pedaling hard against the floor, speeding for a column that stretched too high to see. Please let my theory be right.

I slipped behind it and saw the doorway. A relief until I realized it was barred. The thick door didn't budge when shoved and had no handle to pull. Rather than waste time with it, I sped along the wall, angling for the next column, knowing that expanse I crossed between them left me exposed.

A chill went through me as I heard him counting.

"—five by the dragon gods, six by the dragon gods..."

His version gave me the willies. The next door opened at my shove, and I almost landed face first. I stumbled into a room that held nothing but sconces on the walls. They were lit, I realized, as if someone had been through already. A good sign, as it might be the passage out of this place.

*If I get out, you're a dead man.* Because the first thing I'd do was fetch a gun, and Ward would discover I had a vengeful side when I greeted him with a bullet to the head.

I sprinted across the room to the next door. It led to a staircase that wound up, twirling at least two stories I gauged by the huffing of my breath. How this underground place could be so big boggled the mind. Magic. Had to be.

I emerged into a hallway with doors lining both sides. I shoved. I pulled. Not one would open.

I kept moving, hoping I'd find a clear path out of there, or a better weapon than the puny knife in my hand. A cramp in my midsection had me looking down at my rotund belly. A tummy with an egg inside that Ward wanted to inseminate. I'd not told him about being with Axel the night before. Not mentioned the fact the egg might already be fertilized.

Gulp. *Please don't pull an* Alien *on me.* I'd seen the movie. A horrible way to die.

The hallway of locked doors ended in more stairs, this time going down to a new corridor. The ceiling was high—at least three or more of me high—and wide, too. More sconces lit my path as I headed for the massive metal doors at the far end. Intricate vines covered the metal, and I half expected the door to remain shut. Without me touching it, the portal swung open, and for a second, hope teased me, making me think I'd found a way out.

Nope. Not even close. It appeared I'd found a bedroom, the one place not completely empty. A large bed stood, encased in yellowish amber, and, within that hard material, an actual fucking dragon.

Well holy fucking shit.

I couldn't help but move close to admire the way the solid casing wrapped the very large creature in a thin veneer that preserved it. The dragon appeared to have just gone to sleep. It had to be Satrina. The last dragon. And this was her tomb. Also her legacy. She'd hidden her eggs in this underground lair in the hope of one day having her line live on.

I glanced again at my belly. Surely Ward was wrong. An ancient egg and one night of epic sex surely wasn't enough to bring back a dragon. There had to be a ritual or some vitamins or something more to it. I needed to get my ass to a hospital and demand an extraction before it was too late and my belly exploded.

As I turned from the bed and dragon to see what options I had, I reeled at the sight of Ward. Shirtless, barefoot, and his pants mostly undone. He stalked toward me with a loose long-legged stance that would have been sexy before I realized he was evil incarnate. No longer would I mock the heroine for refusing the hot villain's advances in the movie. I now understood why they said no.

"Found you," he taunted.

"Found but not caught." I clutched the dumb knife and wished I had something bigger.

"Semantics at this point." He lunged, and I reacted, only to realize he feinted.

He flung out his hand and wrapped me in a force shield that kept me from moving. It burned to know he'd toyed with me this entire time. He'd let me run because he knew I was no match for his magic.

A smirk twisted his lips as he stood in front of me. "So much for the fight you promised."

Smug asshole. I wanted to kill him so badly. Instead, I found myself being shoved backwards until I slammed against the hard casing around the dragon. I stuck to the amber like a bug in a web.

Ward grinned. "And now for the main event."

He dropped his pants.

I didn't scream like a damsel but cursed like a sailor. "Keep your raping dick to yourself, you fucking pervert."

"Ooh, threats. I'm so scared," he mocked, getting even closer. He reached to grab hold of the strap on my gown.

My bravery was crushed by my fear. This was it. I'd lost.

A snarl filled the room.

Fuck a knight on a horse. My werewolf had arrived.

# CHAPTER
# TWENTY-ONE

Axel prowled into the room, looking dangerous and furry. His hackles rose in an impressive spine of hair. His head hung low, and his teeth showed as he growled. He took slow, measured steps, the picture of menace.

*Go, Axel!*

I cheered him on mentally and wished he could hear me. It made me ridiculously happy he'd come. He'd chosen to fight for me. Maybe it wasn't too late for us.

Ward crossed his arms as Axel leaped. A force repelled the attack, sending my wolf spinning before he hit the floor and slid. He rose with a shake of his head.

Ward laughed. "Want some more? Or shall we

just end this now? I'll even give you a choice. Dead so you don't have to see me taking her, or alive so you can suffer the guilt of not being able to save her?"

"Grawr."

I didn't speak wolf, but I was pretty sure it was along the lines of fuck off. We were so screwed. We couldn't fight against a warlock's magic.

Maybe if Mindy had been here, she would have provided some protection, but it was just me. Annie, boring human who didn't inherit any cool powers from her parents or distant fae ancestors.

Axel attempted to pounce a few times, only to get more and more frustrated as Ward barely made an effort to deflect.

"Missed me. Missed me, again," Ward taunted.

"Awoo!" Axel howled in frustration.

The situation pissed me off, too. Our lives weren't games, and I was mighty tired of Ward thinking he called the shots. Who was he after all but some pathetic dragon groupie? He wasn't the one carrying an egg. The one who might give birth to a dragon.

Eep.

It wasn't just the birth part that scared the bejesus out of me, but even more frightening would be if Ward got his hands on the dragon. He'd make it into a right psycho killing machine. A bad thing for the population of the world.

Unleashing a people-eating monster wasn't very nice even by my admittedly low standards. So how to get myself out of this situation?

"Enough of this. Time for you to watch while I bring about the new world order." With a wave of Ward's hand, magic enveloped Axel in a bubble, and he floated upward, joining Mungo. Shit, even Jilly was here, eyes open and frantic inside her own force field prison.

The whole gang would watch my shame.

Ward neared, and I knew by his slow walk and dark smile he wanted me afraid.

Instead, I got mad. How dare he think he could touch me? How dare he think he could use me?

No.

I didn't realize the word emerged aloud until Ward's brow raised. "As if you have a choice."

"You're too late. The egg has already been fertilized or whatever you want to call it." As Ward's expression turned to confusion, I clarified. "Last night, while you were busy plotting evil, I was banging a werewolf. Axel is going to be the dragon's baby daddy. Not you."

"Liar!" Ward roared.

"Am I?" I taunted. "Check for yourself and see." I had no idea if it was even possible.

Apparently, Ward thought he could, as he reached for me.

"Don't touch me." I slapped his hand away, once more breaking free without thinking of it.

"Aren't you just full of surprises for a human." Ward grabbed hold of my wrist tight enough to bruise.

My anger exploded, and he yelped, releasing me quickly, probably because my wrist was on fire.

I stared. He stared. We all stared, because what the fuck?

The flames on my flesh went out, and while I didn't have a single blister or even a red burn to show for it, Ward didn't escape unscathed. He held up his hand, charred and oozing, smelling like roasting meat.

"How did you do that?" he asked, grimacing at the pain. I could almost see the magic as he wrapped it in a spell, and the smell of meat disappeared.

I wasn't about to admit I hadn't a fucking clue how I'd done it or if I could do it again. "Come close and I will burn you to a crisp."

A threat that would have worked better if the fire would return. I pointed my hand, shook it, even muttered, "Go, go, fire power!"

The fluke didn't repeat, and Ward regained his cockiness. He swaggered close, leaning right in my face. "Since you're done playing with fire, my turn."

He grabbed me by the crotch and soon regretted it.

"Let me go, asshole!" My rage ignited and lit his hand on fire again, but the flames didn't stop there. Even when Ward pulled his hand free, the fire remained, and it grew, climbing up his arm.

Ward shook it, but that only intensified the flames. Despite his screaming, he remembered to stop, drop, and roll. That only spread the fire to his torso. He staggered to his feet, wheezing and sucking in flames.

He should have died. As if he'd go so easily. He launched himself at me. Still glued to the amber, or perhaps frozen in shock at this point, I didn't move out of the way.

The burning man hit me and huffed, "Die, bitch."

I wanted to say something snappy. I mean, surely there was a retort I could have used, only I found myself distracted as I caught fire!

# CHAPTER
# TWENTY-TWO

I ignited head to toe, and to my shame, I screamed. In my defense, being on fire terrified because, hello, any kind of degree burns hurt. I knew this from experience because of the time I lunged for the marshmallow I was roasting as it fell. In retrospect, not a bright move. I spent that evening in the emergency room instead of making s'mores.

Expecting pain, I hollered, only to realize within seconds the inferno didn't appear to be harming me. Which led to my yodel of terror tapering to a squeak. I stared in fascination. My skin held dancing flames that seemingly did no damage, but my clothes didn't fare as well, dropping from me, the material burning and falling apart to flutter to the floor.

Ward didn't enjoy the same immunity. He'd thrown himself to the floor, tearing at his burning garments and moaning in agony at his bubbling skin. Once more he tried to stop, drop, and roll. It didn't help. He soon ceased moving and just lay there, a burning log of asshole that died.

I knew the moment it happened because the spell on Axel and the others broke. Literally. Axel landed first, on four furry feet. My clumsy Jilly hit in a fluffy heap that bounced to her hooves. As for Mungo, she managed a graceful descent that had her landing on Jilly's back.

A burning pyre, I had no breath to speak, but I did laugh, huffing flame as Axel cocked a leg and peed on the Ward's smoldering corpse.

Kind of jealous. I wouldn't have minded whizzing on the bastard myself, especially given the pressure in my midsection. I glanced down to see my flaming belly expanding. If you've ever seen a horror movie with alien or monster babies that evolve too quickly, then you could picture this.

My tummy went from cantaloupe, to watermelon, to turkey that could feed thirty in the space of seconds.

The belly button protruding had me mentally giggling. *Once it pops it's ready.* Only the oven this turkey planned to emerge from was my vagina, and it definitely lacked the width. There weren't enough

Kegels in the world to save me from what this would do to my cooch.

Yet what choice did I have? My belly rippled, the contraction seizing it and making me gasp as pressure built within my pelvis. I squatted on the floor, still burning bright. A human Axel—very naked and muscled—knelt as close as he could without getting burned.

The flames on my body chose to concentrate on my stomach, meaning I could breathe again and speak. "Oh fuck."

"Button, tell me what I can do to help."

"Don't suppose you have an epidural?" I groaned as my stomach undulated with a contraction.

"I ain't got shit. What's happening?"

"If Ward can be believed, he shoved an ancient dragon egg inside me, which, according to him, just requires sperm to become viable and be born."

"That's impossible." Poor Axel rocked on his heels as I gritted my teeth through a wave of pain.

"That's what I said," I huffed. "But explain this." My belly contorted as if to prove a point.

"This ain't natural, button."

"You don't say." I grunted. The flames intensified, which only made the tensing in my body speed up.

"When you say it needs sperm..." He trailed off, and I gave him the disturbing news.

"Congratulations, you're the daddy."

His eyes widened so far I thought they'd fall out of their sockets.

His shock could wait. "Fuck me, it's coming."

"What do I do?" he asked, despite looking shaken.

"Don't faint."

"Not a time for jokes, button."

"Does this look fucking funny to you?" I yelled as I heaved and pushed.

"We need to get you to a doctor."

"There's no time," I muttered through gritted teeth. The contractions came hard and fast.

I did my best to pant like I'd seen them do on television when pretending to give birth. It didn't help.

It hurt. And whatever was inside wanted out.

So I pushed. And pushed.

A pale Axel knelt between my legs, and when I screamed, "It's coming," he caught what emerged.

# CHAPTER
# TWENTY-THREE

The flames igniting my skin—pretty, wavering tendrils—started out in shades of red, orange, and yellow, but as my body kept contracting, they shifted to blue that faded on the edges into white. The crazy inferno extinguished the moment I gave birth.

To an egg.

Axel, his eyebrows looking singed, held up the gooey oval. The exterior was smooth, which I didn't expect, and an off-white color, if one ignored the goo clinging to it. Disappointing in some respects. I would have expected a dragon egg to be textured and of some epic shade, maybe some sparkle or iridescence?

Not my egg. It came out looking bigger than that

of an ostrich. And FYI, those were pretty freaking big.

"What the fuck?" Axel muttered.

WTF indeed. Then again, why the shock? Technically, all life comes from eggs. Even humans start out that way in a woman's ovary. Fish. Birds. Mammals. Reptiles. Every single one of them involved sperm and an egg. Knowing that didn't make me pushing a large one—and I mean holy-shit sized—out of my cooch an easy thing to deal with. I didn't want to think of the damage done to my tight va-jay-jay. Skewed priorities, perhaps, but better than dealing with the reality.

A fucking egg came out of my body! I'd been used as a surrogate against my will. I had a right to be disturbed.

But I also had a burning question. "Do you think there's a baby inside?"

I didn't think Axel could look more shocked. "I don't know what the fuck this is."

"Dragon egg, according to Ward. Apparently, he used my body as an incubator." I cocked my head and squinted at the ova. "I'm thinking the flames I projected sped up the process."

"Uh." Axel's eloquent reply that finished with his jaw dropped wide enough to catch a swarm of flies.

My naked butt realized I sat on a stone floor. A

heated one but, still, not the best thing. "I don't suppose you brought a blanket or something."

"Uh." Grunted as Axel glanced down at his naked body. Staring would have to wait until later. I had more pressing things to deal with, such as the fact I literally shoved an egg from my tight cooch. No pain didn't mean I wasn't ripped and bleeding. I didn't dare put a hand down there to find out.

"I need something to wear." I stood, still without any discomfort, and managed a smile as Jilly cantered in my direction, a lopsided gait that had Mungo holding on to her single horn lest she get bucked off. "Fluff butt. I'm so glad you and Mungo are okay."

*"Baaa."* Jilly stopped by my side for a rub, and I petted her.

"I was so worried. What a brave goat you are."

Jilly wiggled in reply and somehow loosened the buttons on her pajamas.

"You don't mind me borrowing it?" I asked, helping to remove the fabric.

*"Maaa."*

The swath wasn't big enough to do more than wrap around my waist. It did wonders for my morale though. Now at least I wasn't self-conscious about my coochie wings flapping as I walked.

"That's better," I sang.

Axel might have replied if the egg in his arms didn't wiggle.

He stared. I stared. Jilly and Mungo were super wide-eyed. We all waited for it to move again. Held our breaths in anticipation.

Nothing happened. No Jurassic moment where the cute little dinosaur creature cracks its way out before turning into a bloodthirsty demon. Good thing because I was kind of torn on how to handle it. On the one hand, dragons were historically bad for humanity. On the other, since I'd pushed it out of my body, did that make me the egg's pseudo mama?

Sperm donor, aka father, Axel looked disturbed. "It's alive."

"Yup."

He held it at arm's length. "Should we destroy it?"

"No." I immediately sprang to my egg's defense, even snatching it from his hands. I cradled it to my chest, noting its radiating heat. "How can you even suggest that?"

"Because if that is a dragon, we could save the world a whole lot of strife by acting before it becomes a menace."

"It hasn't even been born, yet you condemn its actions already. What if we can teach it?"

"That isn't a cat or dog or a goat," he reminded. "Dragons are dangerous."

"Says who?"

"Every single story about them."

My lips pursed. "Written by humans who also used to say werewolves should be destroyed."

He shrugged. "They weren't entirely wrong."

"Are you calling yourself evil?"

"No, but I am a killer."

"Do you kill kittens or children?"

"Of course not. And stop changing the subject. We are talking about that." He pointed to the warm egg cradled in my arms.

I nestled my chin atop it. "How can you think of harming whatever is inside? You helped me make life, *Daddy*."

He winced. "Don't say that."

"It's true, though."

"I don't know what the fuck that thing is"—he waved his hand in the egg's direction— "but I can tell you right now, this isn't my baby, or yours."

I recognized his logic and, at the same time, rejected it. The egg, and the life within, was my responsibility. It grew in my body, maybe not for nine months like a human one but I'd nourished this egg. Ruined my tight girly parts to give birth. So what if it might not look like me. I was damned if anyone would hurt my child.

"Maaa."

My gaze flipped to Jilly, who looked rather unsteady. Poor thing appeared bloated all over. Fucking Ward, zapping my almost defenseless goat. Mungo stood by her front legs, wringing her green paws.

"Poor fluffy butt." I rushed to her side, only Jilly shied away, bleating. "I know, you're not feeling too great right now. That's what you get for being so incredibly brave. You saved me."

"Baaa." She uttered a noise of agreement before crookedly cantering for a different door than I'd entered through.

"Your goat's got the right idea. We should get out of here," Axel suggested.

"I agree, but how? This place is a maze. I have no idea where to go."

He snorted. "A maze only if you're using your eyes. Stick with me, button, and I'll get you home."

"Oh I plan to stick close," I muttered. I plastered myself to his body and felt a surprising tingle. Given I'd just shoved a giant egg out of my vagina, that feeling could wait.

"Me lead." Mungo thumped her chest as she strode in the same direction as Jilly trotted. With the egg clutched to my chest, we followed, up and down and around. Just how deep and far underground were we?

The trek took long enough that a quiet Axel finally found the nerve to talk. "Are you okay?"

"Define okay."

He scuffed a bare foot as we walked. "Things got pretty fucked up."

"No shit."

"I didn't mean to upset you back there about the egg and all. I should have realized you'd feel a connection to it."

"I'm surprised you don't. After all, you provided the fertilizer."

"Impossible. I'm a werewolf. I can only mate with my kind or humans."

"According to Ward, dragons can use any kind of sperm. Animal, human, other."

"You're talking about cross-species breeding."

"Which happens all the time. Humans can breed with all kinds of cryptids. Werewolves, witches, demons, fae." I named off the most common.

Axel waved a hand. "All of whom have physical attributes in common, not to mention the same plumbing. Dragons are as far as you can get from human. It shouldn't be possible."

"If it's any consolation, a day ago I would have

agreed. And I usually love a wild theory. At least I understand the whole sperm and egg thing. What I'm having a harder time with is, how did I birth it? How is it I'm not torn in half?" Or so I assumed given the lack of pain or blood. Just a sticky track of goo drying on my inner thighs. So gross. "And where did those flames come from? Was that me or the fucked-up pregnancy hormones?" Either way, I'd wager the extreme heat ripened the egg.

"You handled that remarkably well. Are you sure you're human?"

"They had me tested. And you know my parents. Dad was human all the way, and Mom a weak fae, which means, even if I got a bit of her, it would be like a drop in a sea."

"I don't know what happened," he admitted. "But it was scary as fuck. You were literally a burning pyre."

"It didn't hurt, but it was kind of intense."

"Kind of?" His brows shot up.

How could I explain how transcendent the moment was? I'd felt no pain. No fear once I got over the initial shock. On the contrary, for once in my life, I'd been the heroine of the piece. I vanquished the villain with my very own superpower and then, without any drugs at all and even greater strength, gave birth. Me. After the attack that left me barren,

I'd mourned the fact being a mother was taken from me, and yet now I had an egg that pulsed against my bare chest.

It drew Axel's gaze. "What are you going to do with it?"

"Probably wash it off and then wrap it and put it somewhere." Hidden somewhere it wouldn't get cold or crushed or eliminated by the Cryptid Authority. I had no doubt they'd have the same suggestion as Axel.

"It might not be safe to keep it around."

I pursed my lips. "I am not destroying it."

"Hope you don't live to regret that."

Did Charles Manson's mother regret not getting an abortion? What of all the other mothers of killers? This egg was my only chance at being a mom. I'd love it even if it emerged with a tail. And if it liked to eat fresh meat and blood, well, a farm was the perfect place to raise whatever stirred in the egg. A chunky dragon might not be able to fly and terrorize people. I'd done that to a pony once. Buttercup was a mean one. Once she got too chubby to trot, it became a lot easier to escape her when she decided brushing time was over.

The more we walked that stupid maze, the more I wished I'd found my clothes. Ward must have stashed them somewhere. However, all we saw was bare halls and locked doors. I began to think we were going in circles. My bare feet had enough of slapping stone. A turn of the passage and we hit a staircase going up and, from it, a cool breeze that brought a shiver.

Axel's warm arm around me did much to dispel that cold. I leaned my head on his shoulder.

Maybe everything would be all right.

A hope dashed when the ground began to tremble.

# CHAPTER
# TWENTY-FOUR

Being underground had its challenges. I wasn't a fan of enclosed spaces, but at least the structure appeared solid enough to quell most of my fears. However, the moment I felt shaking I fucking ran. I hit those stairs two at a time, slowing down only because Jilly had some difficulty climbing. Her unwieldy weight gain had her unbalanced and teetering on steps.

Axel murmured, "Move. I'll handle your goat."

Despite her bleat of annoyance, Axel scooped Jilly and slung her across his shoulders. With Mungo leading the way, we hustled. I sweated and panted, the egg jostling in my grip as the tremor underfoot continued. It remained steady and ominous, but the truly terrifying part? The sound of cracking stone.

I'd have peed myself if I wasn't worried about slipping in it.

I huffed and puffed as we climbed those stairs and swore I'd get in better shape. No more ATV around the farm. From now on, I'd walk.

Which did me no good right now.

"Here it comes," Axel muttered. "Keep moving no matter what."

The statement made no sense until the dust cloud hit me. I closed my eyes and mouth against the gritty particles that enveloped us. The rumbling didn't ease but intensified, which gave me a burst of speed.

I was still trying to climb stairs when I realized there was nothing but empty air. I'd reached the top and my wobbly legs almost collapsed under me. I reeled, careening forward, half bent, the egg clutched in my arms until it wasn't.

As it rolled free, I opened my eyes, only to blink at the settling silt. I pushed up on my hands and knees then to my feet.

"Button!" Axel shouted my name.

"Alive!"

My reply guided him through the dirt fog. His hands clutched me, and I clung tight to him. The shiver of the earth underfoot had me pulling back. "We should probably get out of this field."

He laced his fingers with mine and went to move, only I pulled free.

"The egg." I had to bring it with me.

With the dust settling, I could see it lying apparently unharmed only a few paces away. I lunged for it and had almost reached it when the ground gave way.

My scream got cut short as Axel grabbed hold of my arm. He halted my descent into the chasm that opened.

I stared up at him with wide eyes. If he let go—

He heaved me upwards and kept tugging until he had me in his arms. Then he ran, carrying me. A glance over his shoulder showed the egg gone. It was a miracle I'd not disappeared with it given the widening hole.

Axel, busy running, didn't see what shot out next.

I did and managed a not-so-calm scream. "Run faster. Lava!"

Magma spewed from the hole, a fountain up into the sky.

Axel bolted so fast we actually stayed ahead of the disaster and survived. He got us within sight of the farm before he slowed down.

He set me on my feet, and I clung to him. Jilly, who'd somehow managed to keep up with Mungo holding on to her back, leaned against my leg. We all watched the tower of fire spewing into the sky.

It fountained for three days.

Three days where Axel made love to me over and over and over. Partially to ensure my cooch survived the trauma. Luckily, it was if I'd never shoved a giant turkey out of there. I'd been lucky. No stretch marks or ripping or loosey-goosey lips.

When we weren't fucking or farming, Axel and I managed to become the couple we were destined to be. He moved his stuff in from the hotel, and there was no talk of him leaving.

Ever.

I could have held on to my grudge, but at the same time, he'd not been the one to maim me. That was Frenchie. And with her dead, the only person I'd be hurting if I sent him away was myself.

I allowed myself to love.

During the three days of raining magma on the Samson property—because it appeared to be restricted purely to those old boundaries—we had visits from officials. The Cryptid Authority sent someone to make a report. We told them what happened minus a few bits. Axel never once mentioned the egg, so neither did I.

We did, however, tell them about Ward and the fact he'd not made it out of the lair that collapsed when the underground lava flow got too pressurized and exploded. Or at least we assumed he died. Never did find a body.

The CA then told us Ward had been fired from the Cryptid Historical Society. Apparently, he'd been caught stealing relics from the dragon age. A man obsessed and I still didn't fully understand his logic in that respect.

The spewing magma ended on the third day. Once the ground cooled enough, we weren't the only ones to put on some thick boots and go exploring. All kinds of government groups went traipsing that following week. Not that there was much to see. The Samson place was a hellish wasteland of cooling lava, burned trees and ground, and a crater forming a pool of bubbling magma.

The total lack of life didn't stop the Cryptid Authority from slapping a condemnation notice on the property. No farming, no trespassing. They declared the whole place off-limits and bought it from me for twice what I paid.

The ink on the deal hadn't even dried when I went for a walk.

"I'll come with you," Axel offered.

I shook my head. "I just need a minute to process the fact I'm losing my dream." So much for expanding the farm. I headed off on foot, walking farther than I'd planned while, at the same time, knowing exactly where I was going.

There was a fence barring my path. It didn't need a sign given the hair on my body lifted as I neared. The spell on the boundary ensured I didn't disobey the no-trespassing promise I'd signed. It couldn't stop me from walking the line between my land and the property next door.

Last night, I'd dreamed about the Samson place, imagined I visited and sat by the edge of the crater, singing in a weird language.

Just a dream. I'd woken that morning in bed, still naked beside Axel, my feet unblemished and clean.

I stopped a moment in front of the fence and stared beyond. While I'd not dreamed of the egg, I'd been thinking of it. Wondering what happened to it.

As I turned around to go home, I noticed a thread of steam rising from the pasture that next spring would grow the wheat grass I'd seeded. I headed for the mist, which increased in thickness as pressure pushed it out of the ground. A part of me warned I should run away, but my feet kept moving toward it instead. The crack in the earth widened and formed a lip, almost a basin, from which emerged the top of an egg.

My egg.

Before my dumb ass could register the bad

idea, I'd placed my hand on it. The heat radiated enough to burn, only my skin simply tingled. I cocked my head as the shell under my palm vibrated.

"Come on, baby," I crooned. "Come to Mama."

The knocking inside the shell increased, and cracks webbed its surface.

I wanted to help, but being a farmer, I understood nature. The shell began to push outward as chunks of it were shoved free. A clawed paw poked through then retreated. It emerged in another spot, quickly followed by a head.

The baby dragon emerged from the shell, a thing of moist, leathery skin, a pale gray in color. Its eyes were pure black. It stared at me and opened its mouth.

It croaked, and before I could reply, I was pulled back.

"Get behind me," Axel ordered. He held a gun.

"What are you doing?" I popped to my feet in front of him.

"It's a dragon, button. You heard what all those officials told us."

All dragons were to be exterminated on sight.

"I don't care. That's our baby. Mine and yours."

"Button..." he pleaded.

"Please, Axel."

He sighed. Heavily. "If we keep it, someone will find out."

"I know. Guess it's a good thing you work for the CA and can make sure that doesn't happen." Perhaps it wasn't fair, but I did it anyhow. "You owe me."

Before he could agree, junior had shoved out of its shell and stretched its wings.

I couldn't help but smile. "Hi, baby! Come see your mama." I held out my arms.

It hissed in my direction before flapping. It took a running start, jumped, and lifted off the ground.

Leaving home already. They grew up so quick.

The baby dragon flew away.

Axel put his arm around my shoulders. "Probably for the best."

My lips pursed. "Don't make me hurt you."

"Hurt me all you like so long as you never leave me." He cupped my head and drew me close for a kiss. "I love you, button."

I loved him, too, although I did wonder how that love would work. I was a farmer. He wasn't. Yet, as the days passed, Axel stuck around, helping out around the farm while still doing odd jobs for the Cryptid Authority. Apparently, our little geographic area had become some kind of hotspot for weird shit. Folks claimed to have seen all kinds of stuff in and around town.

Sasquatch. Little people with wings that glowed all kinds of colors. Even a centaur on the loose. That caused some skepticism given it appeared male but didn't have a long dong. What no one had spotted? One stubby-horned goat. Jilly went missing not long after baby Hiss was born. One morning we woke to not find her and her fat belly splayed across the foot of our bed. I looked everywhere for her. Even Axel helped out by using his nose. Literally.

It was as if she'd vanished.

I wasn't the only one missing a pet. Mungo also went AWOL, but Mindy seemed unbothered. "Did you know goblins go into heat?" she confided. "You ain't seen disturbing until you've seen one dry humping a cob of corn. Who does that?"

Something looking for textured ridges. Not that I needed to rely on vegetables or artificial sexual devices. I had the real deal. A lover who satisfied me every night in bed, the field, the barn, behind the barn... And before you think Axel kept mauling me all over the place, let me set you straight. I did most of the initiating. I'd see that beautiful man bent over and couldn't resist.

But back to Jilly. I worried about her, but as Axel

reminded me, "This is her home. She'll be back when she's ready."

Unless she'd gone somewhere to die. Animals did that when they felt their end nearing, and no doubt there'd been something off about Jilly. I'd tried to get her to see the vet, only she disappeared before the appointment.

I hoped she was okay.

Just like I hoped Hiss thrived. In case my baby ever came home, I switched the focus on Earth's Bounty to a meatier kind of stock. After all, a fat dragon fed at home couldn't hurt anyone.

I farmed. I loved. I lived.

Happily ever after. Even if Axel wouldn't let us have a cute couple name like Anxel.

# EPILOGUE

Axel freely admitted he'd fucked up when he was young, hence screw waiting this time. Within a month of reuniting with his only love, he married Button at town hall only two days after proposing. Despite the short notice, Annie managed to put him in a blue ruffled tux. He looked ridiculous, although, if she'd demanded it, he would have worn a clown suit or even pointy-toed cowboy boots. He would have given her the world. Thankfully, all she wanted was him.

Mindy and Reiver acted as their witnesses. Axel's bride wore her newest favorite T-shirt under her cleanest overalls. He'd had the top custom made with an intricate flying serpent and captioned it Mother of Dragon, a beast they'd not seen since its release. Although he had his suspicions given Annie had increased their livestock herds, which oddly led to them losing more of them to incidentals.

But he wasn't about to do or say anything about it. After all, the dragon was the only child they'd ever have. He just hoped it never caused the kind of trouble that would force them to choose sides, because no way would he ever betray Annie again.

After the wedding, followed by cake and the best damned bread he'd ever eaten, they returned to the farm, whereupon Axel carried his bride over the threshold.

"We're home, wife."

She giggled. "I don't know if I'm ready to hear you call me that."

"Too bad, you'll be hearing it a lot. Wife. Wifey poo. Or would you prefer ball and chain?"

"You know your dad will be pissed about it."

"My father can go piss on a hydrant," he said, which made her laugh.

What she didn't know, because she'd been out with Mindy that day, was his father had shown up at the farm within days of Axel moving in with Annie. Given him an ultimatum.

*"I'll give the Pack to your cousin if you don't get rid of the woman."*

*"I'm not leaving Annie."*

*"She's human."*

*"And?"*

*"And she can't even give you children."*

*"She gives me something more important."*

Love. Peace. The life he'd always wanted and spent more than twenty years missing out on.

"You say the sexiest things," Annie teased, nipping at his jaw.

"I'm about to do even sexier stuff, wife," he uttered in a low growl. He carried Annie into the bedroom and stopped dead.

"What is it? Fuck..." Annie blinked at the sight of her bed, which would probably need to be burned. Or at the very least end up as a research subject for a Cryptid lab because there was a unicorn nestled in their bed.

How the unicorn got inside, he couldn't have said, and why it chose their—

The unicorn rose and stepped lightly to the floor, sides heaving and writhing.

"What's wrong with it?" he asked, his hand inching for the gun at his side, debating if he should swap into fur.

That was when the missing Mungo popped up, clinging to the unicorn's mane. The goblin had one word. "Baby."

"Holy shit, it's giving birth!" Annie yelled. Did she run away from the anomaly in her bedroom?

Nope, she went to her knees by the unicorn's tail to help. "Get me some towels," she barked.

"This wasn't the wedding night I imagined," he grumbled as he fetched on command.

It took some heaving and whinnying before an egg plopped from the unicorn, with Mungo trying to catch it and getting flattened. Annie saved the goblin by grabbing the slimy-looking ova, only to squeak as it moved in her grip. She quickly set it down on the floor then stepped back.

"What is it?" Axel whispered.

"I don't know."

"Is it another dragon egg?" The sphere was not the size, shape or even color as the one that hatched the dragonling. Ward would have known but the fucker was dead. Had he implanted more eggs than they'd realized? That would be a clusterfuck and a half if true.

Annie squinted at the ova. "Looks like it could be another dragon. Should we drop it on one of the heat vents and see if it hatches?"

"No dragon," Mungo interrupted. "Baby." The goblin patted the egg. It began to crack. The outer crunchy layer flaked off leaving an undulating sac that rippled with motion.

"The baby is caught in a birthing shroud. It needs help." Annie didn't shy away but tore at the membrane with her bare hands, revealing the foal within. The baby wobbled its way out of the casing and stood on spindly legs.

The unicorn leaned its head down to nuzzle. The baby leaned against its mother, a nub of a horn on its head, its coat a fuzzy white, its eyes like big round jewels. The leathery wings folded down its back proved to be a surprise.

And of course Annie clapped her hands and exclaimed, "Isn't it just beautiful!"

"Maaa." The unicorn agreed but the noise appeared to startled Annie.

She stared and uttered a soft, "Jilly, is that you?"

The head bobbed. "Maaa."

Annie reached out to stroke her muzzle. "But how?" How had a goofy goat turned into a graceful unicorn?

"Curse." Mungo supplied the answer. "Bad spell. Broken."

"How?"

"Magic kiss." The goblin's smacking lips didn't seem too magical to Axel, but hey, no arguing the result.

"I'm just glad you're all right." Annie flung her arms around the goat who wasn't a goat. A second later she included the foal who was more than a foal.

It was only as Jilly settled in the bed, the baby nursing from her and Mungo perched with them, beaming, that it hit Axel who had impregnated Jilly. Which meant remembering what he'd learned about goblins. Essentially, if needed, they could swap out their sex organs, a species-saving trait.

"We should let them rest."

It was only as Annie tugged him out of the room that he protested. "Our wedding night deserves a bed."

"Our wedding night just needs us naked." She winked. "I have something better than a regular ol' bed."

Once they threw a blanket down on a mound of hay in the barn, it made a great spot to make love. More than once. They barely got any sleep on their wedding night, but he did howl, and when she rubbed that one special spot, he couldn't stop his leg from thumping.

A dragon might have its hoard, and a Pack its outdated rules, but Axel had love, and this time, he'd tear anyone apart before he ever gave it up.

The next morning, when he woke to see a baby dragon eyeing them both, before Annie could even ask, he was rolling out of the hayloft saying, "I'll fetch it some meat from the fridge."

After all, he was the father of a dragon, and a daddy should always protect his baby girl.

THE END OF ANNIE'S STORY. I HOPE YOU LOVED IT BECAUSE ONCE I MET ANNIE IN EARTH'S DAUGHTER, I JUST HAD TO GIVE HER A HAPPILY EVER AFTER. BUT WE'RE NOT DONE. TAKE A LOOK AT WHAT'S NEXT ~ EARTH'S ELF. (AND YES, THAT IS AN EVIL GINGERBREAD ON THE COVER).

*For more Eve Langlais books visit EveLanglais.com*

www.ingramcontent.com/pod-product-compliance
Lightning Source LLC
LaVergne TN
LVHW031540060526
838200LV00056B/4583